TRAIL
NUMBER FOUR

Janice N. Chapman

ISBN 978-1-956010-04-6 (paperback)
ISBN 978-1-956010-05-3 (digital)

The characters in this book are purely fictional.

Janice N. Chapman
2118 Oak Street
Harper, Kansas 67058

Rushmore Press LLC
1 800 460 9188
www.rushmorepress.com

Printed in the United States of America

Acknowledgments

I would like to thank Dr. Holly Kathryn Norton, PhD, of the Office of Archaeology and Historic Preservation in Colorado for her assistance and invaluable archaeology information on the research I needed for this book.

1

They had walked all day in light snow. It was cold, and they were weary. They had not found what they were looking for, and it was getting late. It was time to go back to the cabin, get warmed up, and drink some hot chocolate.

"I think it's time to go to the cabin. All in favor say *aye*!" Curtis shouted.

His two brothers and his two boys shouted *aye* together, and it echoed from the sides of the canyons. They laughed as they listened to the echoes of their voices, and they turned and started back toward the cabin. The trees were edged in white where the snow had settled on them, making them look like a magical forest. The tracks they had made earlier that morning were no longer visible to them. The boys wanted to run, but Curtis vetoed the idea. If they were to fall in this fresh snow, they could get hurt badly. The snow was soft, but the ground beneath it was frozen and hard and they didn't need any broken bones.

They had walked farther than any of them had realized, and by the time they reached the cabin, it was almost dark. The warmth inside was welcome, even though the old open-faced wood-burning stove was sorely in need of more wood.

Chance, Curtis's oldest brother, offered to bring in more wood and fill the wood box.

"Can I help?" his ten-year-old nephew Taylor asked.

"Sure. Come on," replied his uncle.

Woody, the second-oldest brother, took off his wraps and gloves and hung them on one of the pegs on the cabin wall just inside the door. His nephew Lorne did the same thing with his wraps and gloves.

Curtis poured water into the coffee pot and set it on top of the stove into which he put two chunks of wood. He would make the hot chocolate as soon as the water was hot enough.

Chance and Taylor came inside with armfuls of cut-up wood from the side of the cabin and laid it in the wood box that had been built for that purpose. Chance opened the front of the stove and put three pieces of the wood inside and closed the door on the stove. It crackled and popped as the fire melted the snow from the frozen wood. Next he built a fire in the fireplace. He and his ten-year-old nephew Taylor both removed their wraps and gloves and found a place to sit down.

Curtis was busy mixing cocoa in with sugar into which he then mixed the hot water from the coffeepot. Woody found cups for all of them to enjoy the hot liquid.

"Tomorrow," Curtis told them, "we'll go east and see what we can find and maybe bring down a deer too, if we get a chance. Even though I didn't see any of those today."

Who ever had built the cabin before the Demming brothers bought the land had built it well. It was a large two-bedroom cabin. It hosted a fireplace, a woodburning stove, and a woodburning cookstove. It also had an indoor water pump. The only thing lacking was electricity and enough beds for all of them. Curtis, Chance, and Woody had bought some cots at a local sporting goods store and had purchased extra bedding and pillows at the local mercantile store, along with some canned goods and paper plates and cups to use at the cabin. They also bought a garbage can and a box of garbage bags to use at the cabin. There was an outdoor outhouse too, which they furnished with toilet paper.

Chance set about cleaning his rifle in case they might run across a deer or a pronghorn on tomorrow's journey. His nephews watched and drank their cocoa. Woody and Curtis had also seated themselves at the table.

"Can I have some more cocoa?" asked Taylor.

"Sure, Taylor. It looks like the rest of us could use some refills too," his Dad told him as he got up to get the pot of cocoa.

He was sure Taylor could have carried it, but he didn't want to take a chance on Taylor spilling any of it on anyone.

"Is anyone hungry?" Woody asked them. "Or are you too tired to eat right now?"

"I can eat anytime," Lorne told his uncle.

Uncle Woody laughed at him but turned to see what goodies were lurking among the canned goods.

"Looks like sandwiches and chicken noodle soup," he told them.

He heard no complaints, so he fixed the sandwiches while the soup was heating.

"Hey, boys, it would be a good idea if we pick up a cooler and some ice next time we go to town. Then we would have something to put a few cold cuts and maybe some bacon in."

"And maybe some sodas for these two young sprouts," Curtis added.

Chance put his rifle aside and lit the lamps for them. "We probably need to pick up some extra oil for these lamps and some extra rifle shells."

His brothers agreed with him. Curtis got down bowls for Woody to put their soup in and handed out spoons to them. Woody put their sandwiches on paper plates for them. And opened two sleeves of crackers.

"Looks fit for a king!" Chance commented.

"Well, then we three Demming kings and our two Demming princes shall partake of this wondrous 'fit for a king' meal," Woody mocked his brother.

He made a mock bow before he sat down to enjoy his own bowl of soup and his sandwich.

"This is good, Uncle Woody," Lorne told him.

"I'm glad you like it," his Uncle Woody said.

"Did you boys bring your games with you?" Curtis asked his boys.

Both of them had handheld games they played religiously at home when they were bored with everything else.

"I did," said Lorne.

"I brought mine too," Taylor told him, holding his game up for his dad to see.

"That's good because we don't have electricity in the cabin. So no TV out here," Curtis stated. "I brought an extra deck of playing cards in case you boys want to play cards."

To his brothers, he asked, "Either of you interested in a game of Pitch?"

Chance and Woody both accepted, and they played for nearly three hours before giving it up. By then, the boys had already gone to bed. Each of the men also found a cot, turned out the lamps, and were soon asleep.

The snow had stopped but left a white cloud of fog across the timbered land. It left a ghostly shroud of light across the stillness of the night. It hung like a shroud over the cabin and the truck.

* * * * *

Curtis woke early before any of the others. He lit a lantern and started coffee. Opening the door, he was surprised at how serene the scene before him was. He walked to the outhouse with a feeling of complete peace, and returning to the house, the same feeling came over him. It could stay like this forever, and he'd be content.

When he stepped inside the cabin, Woody was stirring.

He yawned and stretched and asked his brother, "So we want to go east today, Curtis? How about if we write down which trails we have explored?"

"That's a good idea, Woody. We can tack it on the door. Yesterday we walked south, so I guess it would be Trail Number One," Curtis replied as he poured both of them cups of coffee. "I thought we'd go east today into that rocky canyon and see what we can find. We'll have to be careful because those rocks will be slippery. This fog should burn off by ten or ten thirty. By then, we should have good visibility. And if we run across a deer or antelope, maybe we can have steaks for supper."

"Who's worried about steaks? Some flapjacks would work wonders right about now," Woody said as he headed to the outhouse.

Chance got up and poured himself a cup of coffee and joined Curtis at the table.

"Looks like the snow quit," he commented.

A cold blast of air punctuated his statement as Woody opened the door and came in.

"Have you seen the fog this morning?" Woody asked.

When his brother Chance told him no, Woody said, "It's eerie! It gives everything a ghostly look. I hope it burns off soon."

"Eerie, huh?" Chance chided. "You aren't a little bit spooky this morning are you, Woody?"

Their voices woke the boys who yawned and stretched and tumbled out of their beds not quite awake.

"What we havin' for breakfast?" Lorne mumbled.

"I thought I might stir up some flapjacks as soon as everybody's awake," his dad told him.

"Make lots of them cause I'm starved," Lorne returned.

"Me, too," Taylor told him as he and his brother shuffled toward the table.

The men laughed at them. Ten- and twelve-year-old's had hollow toes, and the walk yesterday made them hungrier than usual.

The pancakes Curtis served everyone hit the spot, and they ate heartily. He made some extra pancakes to take with them today in case the boys got hungry before they returned to the cabin in the evening.

He made sure the boys had gone to the outhouse and made up their cots before leaving the cabin. Chance also visited the outhouse and checked his rifle again.

When they were all outside he asked, "Which way we headin' this morning?"

"I thought we'd go east today down that canyon and see what we can scare up for meat. We could possibly find what we're lookin' for down in that canyon, too."

"Suits me," Chance told him.

Visibility was getting better the farther they walked. As they neared the entrance of the canyon, Curtis told his boys to be careful, especially on the rocks because they would be slippery from the fog that was just now burning off of them.

Woody stopped and motioned to Chance and pointed to his right. Behind a scrub oak stood a deer. Chance maneuvered his rifle slowly to his shoulder and fired. The deer fell.

They all walked over to the tree to see where the deer fell. It was a young buck.

"You got him, Uncle Chance!" quipped Taylor. "You got him!"

"I'll help you field dress him," Woody offered.

With that done, they carried the deer back to the cabin. There they skinned him and cut him into quarters and put the meat in some of the garbage bags Curtis had brought with him. For want of a cooler, Curtis climbed on top of the cab of his truck and swung the bags on top of the cabin roof. Climbing down from on top of his truck, he then backed it a little ways away from the cabin. He didn't think wolves or coyotes could get at the meat he just put on top of the cabin. Most of the bears had gone into hibernation. So unless a lynx or a mountain cat wandered by, their meat supply should be safe. They folded the hide and put it into a bag also but set it inside the cabin for now.

"Shall we wash up and try this again?" Curtis asked.

"Yeah, brother. Now that we have our steaks for supper secured, let's get back out there and see what else we can find."

2

Noon was closing in, and some of the snow had melted. The east trail was more rocky near the edges and walls of the canyon, and it boasted an abundance of the Ponderosa pine native to that area of Colorado. There were some lodgepole pines amid the stand of trees. Aspens farther out lent to the scenery their beautiful orange and gold leaves, although most of the leaves had already fallen from them.

"Look how tall those trees are!" exclaimed Taylor. "I sure wouldn't want to climb one of those trees!"

"You'd have to have a spring board to reach the lower limbs even!" Lorne stated.

A little further on, they found a place to descend into the canyon. There were a few rocks along the descent and Curtis warned his sons to be very careful going down.

Once on the canyon floor, all of them gazed momentarily at the beauty of the canyon area. Even with un-melted snow, the canyon held a magnificent view in all directions. Curtis was glad he brought the boys along. This was their first time to be a part of such an excursion. So far, they seemed in awe of this beautiful land he and his brothers bought.

He and his brothers all hunted in lands of this sort as young boys while growing up, and when this land became available, the three of them went in together to buy it. Now the boys could enjoy it as much as the men did. They were out of school now for the Thanksgiving holidays, so they had ample time to explore it now with their father and their two uncles.

The five of them began walking eastward. Chance stopped after a few yards, bringing his rifle to his shoulder.

The rest stopped also, and Curtis asked his brother, "What do you see?"

"Quiet!" Chance whispered. "I've got a ram in my sight. I just need him to turn a bit to get a kill shot!"

They stood like frozen statues while waiting for the ram to turn from the position he was in when Chance first spotted him. Finally, he did turn, and Chance fired. The report was loud in the canyon, and it echoed back to them. They walked to where the ram lay. They field dressed it and carried it back to the cabin, skinned it, and quartered the meat the same as they had done the deer. Once bagged in the garbage bags, Curtis moved his truck to where he could climb on to the cab and throw the ram meat on top of the cabin roof.

He wondered why the ram had wandered into this area. Perhaps he had gotten separated from the herd or had gotten caught in a storm and driven here.

No matter, he told himself, *we'll be good eating tonight.*

"I'm in favor of going to town and getting some coolers. We could take the deer meat in to the Processing Plant in Pueblo and have them cut it up for us," Curtis suggested.

It was thirty-eight miles to the Processing Plant in Pueblo, but it was the nearest one.

"That's a good idea," Woody told him.

Chance agreed also, and they washed the blood off their hands.

"What are you going to do with the ram?" Taylor asked.

"Leave him here for now," his dad answered. "We may take him to the Processing Plant later on."

"Can we come back here, Dad? I'd like to see some more of this place. Besides, we haven't been west or north on it yet. And I bet there are some pretty places in those directions too," Lorne spoke with expectancy.

They walked back to the cabin. Curtis Demming pulled his vehicle forward, climbed onto the cab of his truck, pulled the deer meat down, and laid it in the bed of his truck. It had frozen overnight on top of the roof. By morning, the ram meat would be frozen too. But they needed things from town, so for now, he only took the deer meat.

He got down from the top of his pickup and on down to the ground. Then he asked his boys and his brothers if they were ready to go. They were, and they started loading into the pickup.

"Wait!" called Lorne. "I've got to tie my shoe!"

They waited on him, and moments later, they were all in the pickup and headed for town.

At the Meat Processing building, Curtis went inside and found an employee. It was nearly closing time, but when Curtis explained about the deer in his pickup, the man told him to bring it on in.

"I have a mountain ram back at the cabin that I'll bring in tomorrow," he told the clerk.

"That's fine. We can cut up both of them for you and have them ready for you to pick up in a couple of days," the clerk told him. He did not seem a bit surprised that Curtis had a ram.

"That's great. By then, the boys will have to be back in school. I may need to rent a locker too. I don't think Megan has room in the freezer for both of them," Curtis replied.

Megan was his wife. She put up with him and their boys like a saint. Rarely did he hear her raise her voice to any of them. She wouldn't win any beauty contests, but she didn't need to. She had an inner beauty that she graciously handled them with on a daily basis. She cooked and cleaned and looked after him and their boys with the patience of Job. He told himself he could not have found a better woman to share his life with.

Chance and Woody had never married. Woody had considered it once, but the relationship fizzled out before it ever got to the altar, leaving Woody sullen for a long time. But eventually, he came back to his old self, much to the relief of all concerned. Chance was the sportsman of the three brothers and more restless than either Woody or Curtis. Tall and lanky with a grin that could woo any of the girls he had been around, he had remained aloof, not wanting any of their attention for long. Both of them loved Megan like a sister rather than a sister-in-law. Maybe their singleness was because they had not found a woman that equaled Megan's standards. None of them drank to speak of. Now and then a can of Coors or a bottle of Miller Lite, but that wasn't too often.

He went back to the pickup and drove down to the Mercantile store a couple blocks away. There he gave Lorne and Taylor each a five-dollar bill to spend while he and their uncles did their shopping for things they all needed back at their cabin. Curtis picked up a large cooler and inspected it. Satisfied it was the size they needed, he bought two of them—one he would use as a refrigerator for goods that had to be kept cool and the other he would use for meat so he didn't have to continue throwing it onto the roof of the cabin. He could have the boys scoop up the snow and make it into snowballs that would freeze outside and would be used in the coolers in place of ice cubes.

He bought oil for the lanterns, matches, extra shells for Chance's rifle, canned goods, and what staples they were short on. And then because he knew Megan didn't have a spare one at the house, he bought a Dutch oven they could use to make soup in.

Chance thought to buy a snow shovel in case they needed to shovel a path to the outhouse or shovel a place behind his vehicle if they had to shovel snow out of the way to get out of where he had been parking it. Curtis had snow chains, but for deep snow, they still might need the shovel. Woody found some rope and masking tape and some candles and an armload of junk food he thought his nephews would enjoy.

"Hey, Dad! Look what we found!" exclaimed Taylor, coming through the door of the store.

Lorne and Taylor bought some comic books and necessary things like candy and chewing gum and popcorn.

Curtis was a bit surprised at the comic books. He had not observed his boys reading those, but maybe they thought it would give them something to do at the cabin since they had no electricity there and couldn't watch TV programs they usually enjoyed.

"Looks like that will keep you busy for a while," he smiled at them, and so did their uncles.

Electricity might be a project for him and his brothers to pitch in together next year to pay for having it strung out to and installed in the cabin. Right now, the boys were happy with what they had bought for themselves, and that was what mattered. He was happy for them.

"You boys about ready to stop by and see your mom before we go back to the cabin?"

Curtis's house was just outside of town on the northern side. It was a four-bedroom, two-bathroom structure with a large yard, both front and back, with a medium-sized toolshed to one side of the backyard.

They piled out of his pickup in his driveway at his house, and Megan met him at the door.

"Why are you guys home so early?" she asked.

Curtis gave her a hug then made room for Lorne and Taylor to hug her too.

"I came by to tell you we dropped off a deer at the Processing Plant in Pueblo, and tomorrow I will bring in the ram Chance shot. The clerk said both will be ready in a couple of days," her husband answered.

"Oh, Curtis! I don't know if we have room in the freezer for both of them," she said.

"I told the clerk I might need to rent a locker from them, so don't worry, Megan. At least we have meat for this winter. And knowing Chance, he's apt to bring down whatever else gets in front of the sights on his rifle if he thinks we need it."

Megan hugged him and gave him a kiss. "How are the boys liking it out there in the country?"

"They are doing all right. Right now, it's new to them. They've got both their uncles with them. So it's exciting to them, except for not having a TV to watch," Curtis told her.

Both boys came back into the room carrying a few more items to take back to the cabin with them. Curtis reminded them to use the bathroom. They laid the few items they carried on the floor and, in a few minutes, came back to retrieve them.

Megan kissed them both on the cheek, gave them a quick hug, and told them she loved them and to enjoy their weekend.

We will, Mom. We love it out there! Next time you'll have to come with us!" Taylor told her.

Megan smiled at hers son's excitement.

"Maybe by then I can," she agreed.

Curtis gave her a hug and followed the boys back to the vehicle where their uncles waited.

3

That evening while Curtis fixed their supper, Lorne and Taylor busied themselves reading their new comic books. Funny, Curtis thought, how flexible kids can be. At home TV was king, but without TV, other things quickly removed the king from his throne.

Chance cleaned his rifle, and Woody readied the table for their supper.

"You guys get ready for supper," Curtis told them.

"You know," Woody said, "I should have bought a new skinning knife while we were in town. Remind me tomorrow when we take the ram in to the Processing Plant to get one. And a whet stone too."

"I thought you did pretty good with the one you have," Chance told him.

"It does okay," Woody admitted. "But a new one will do better."

"Maybe all it need is a good sharpening," Chance offered.

He hadn't noticed his brother with a whet stone lately, and his belt had remained around his waist. He figured Woody just wanted a new knife.

"Tomorrow is another day. I might see about getting Lorne and Taylor each a good pocket knife. They're both old enough to learn to use one," Curtis commented.

"You mean it, Dad?" Taylor asked excitedly.

"Yes, I mean it. You and Lorne are both old enough to learn to use a knife. But you absolutely cannot take them to school with you. Your Uncle Chance and Uncle Woody and myself will all be a part of the learning of how to use your knives," Curtis answered.

"Dad, you're the greatest!" Lorne exclaimed.

"When one of us tells you something, you need to pay attention," Woody told them. "Getting careless or reckless with a knife can get you killed. They're not toys. They're tools."

"We'll be careful, Uncle Woody," Taylor told his uncle.

"If you don't, I'll bust your butts for you. Your Dad won't have to," Chance assured them.

Both his nephews looked at him and knew he meant what he'd said.

Curtis smiled, but he knew his brother wouldn't hesitate to carry out his threat to his nephews. Time would tell whether either of them—hopefully both of them—would grow up to be a good woodsman. At ten and twelve, they were both old enough to pay attention and still young enough to not fully understand the meaning of *careless* and *reckless*. He was sure they would learn but not all at once in the next two days. It would take a few years for them to learn the specifics about knives and their uses and their care. But tomorrow would be their beginning in knife education.

It seemed to him that all of them were hungrier than usual. The excitement of the last two days, the killing of the deer and the ram, and the atmosphere in the Colorado hills caused all their appetites to grow. They slept better at night too. He was glad he and his brothers had decided to go ahead and buy this piece of land.

Woody elected to cook breakfast. Now that they had coolers in which to keep food cool, they could have breakfast meat—bacon, ham, or sausage—with their eggs. And he could fix pan-fried toast to butter and/or eat with jelly. He whistled as he worked. He hadn't done that in a long time. He didn't know why he did it now, but he felt like whistling, so he did.

"You sound happy this morning, Uncle Woody. I haven't heard you whistle a tune in a long time. You ought to do it more often," Taylor told him.

His Uncle Woody laughed at him.

"And you ought to laugh more often too," his nephew Lorne informed him.

Kids! God love 'em! Woody thought, glad they were his nephews.

He quit whistling and set breakfast on the table while the boys set the dishes and tableware on it.

Immediately after breakfast, they loaded the ram quarters into the truck and took it to the Processing Plant in Pueblo. Curtis took the ram meat inside.

"How much do your lockers run?" Curtis asked the clerk.

"They run forty-five dollars a month," the clerk told him.

"Make me out a receipt for one then," Curtis said as he pulled cash from his wallet.

The clerk wrote the receipt and put the money in the register. He gave Curtis a key to the meat locker, along with the number of it. It was to one of the large lockers and should hold anything Chance could bring down with his rifle.

He went back to his pickup and drove down the street to the Mercantile. All of them got out and walked inside.

"Where do you keep your knives?" Curtis asked the owner.

"Right over here," the man told him, leading the way to a locked glass cabinet in which he kept a nice display of knives. "Can I get some out for you to look at?"

His brothers and his sons had already started looking at the display.

"I want to get the boys each a pocket knife," Curtis told him. "And my brother here wants a new skinning knife."

"You'll probably want the Case pocket knives. They're the best on the market right now," the clerk told him, picking up two of the knives and laid them on top of the counter.

Curtis opened one and checked it over, then laid it down and picked up the second knife and inspected it.

Laying it back on the counter, he asked Taylor and Lorne, "Do you boys like these knives?"

Both answered yes excitedly.

"Pick the ones you want and look them over," he told them. "But be careful. Those blades are sharp."

They both picked up a knife and opened the blades and looked the knife they held over, then closed the blades. Curtis asked if they were sure those were the knives they wanted, and they both said yes. Case was top of the line in pocket knives, and he wanted them to have good ones.

Woody found a new bowie knife he liked and asked the clerk to see it. The clerk put the Bowie into its sheath and handed it to Woody. Woody took it out of the sheath carefully and looked it over, feeling the edge of the blade for sharpness. Satisfied it was what he wanted, he put it back in the sheath and asked the merchant for a whet stone also and a small can of oil to use on the whet stone.

By that time, Chance had found a scrapper with which he liked to use to scrap the hides. He bought two and some nails and a hammer to tack the hides to the side of the cabin where they would scrape them, and when they were done with that, they would salt the hides to help keep them soft and to preserve them. He would later show his nephews how to scrap the skins so they didn't damage them or at least would have minimal damage from beginning students.

They got back to the cabin just before noon. None of them were hungry, so they decided to try walking to the north. The boys put their new pocket knives in the pockets of their jeans. Somehow, carrying knives in their pockets put them a bit higher on the growing-up scale. They had become big boys now instead of just boys. Curtis thought they both walked a little prouder.

The northern area of their property hosted a nice meadow with grass still showing some green toward the bottom of the blades. It had a small stream running east and west through it where the wildlife could come and drink. It was home to some of the pine and blue spruce, and Curtis also saw a few cedars and a few small shrubs amid the tree area. It was a beautiful view to behold, a place he himself could spend hours just looking at the scenery, and at the Green Mountains that loomed to the northwest of where they were walking, and at the Sangre de Cristo Mountains that enveloped the west and southwest as far as the eye could see.

The stream was barely ten inches wide in some places, and it widened out in other places. It was fed by a natural spring as well as the snow melting run off from the mountains farther on.

"We need to get us some gold-hunting pans!" Lorne said.

"Yeah! There's probably some gold nuggets in that stream!" his brother agreed.

The menfolk laughed at them.

"I doubt very much if there's any gold in that stream. There might be some fool's gold that's washed down from the mountains. But probably nothing worth keeping except as souvenirs," Curtis told them.

"Well, if we do find some can we keep it?" Lorne asked him.

"Sure. And there might be some other type mineral rocks you will want to collect too."

He smiled at his son. He heard Chance and Woody chuckling behind him. He wouldn't be a bit surprised if both of his brothers helped Lorne and Taylor's rock collection along.

For lack of seeing any wildlife at this time of day, they walked along the bank of the stream for a ways, giving the boys ample time to feast their eyes on the streambed, checking for treasures as they walked a ways in front of their dad and their Uncles. After a few minutes, Taylor spotted a rock he wanted and bent down to retrieve it from the streambed.

"What's this?" he asked, showing it to the men.

"Looks like it may be some type of quartz," Uncle Chance told him. "Probably a little piece of white quartz."

Woody and Curtis both thought so too.

"Can I keep it?" Taylor asked.

"Yes, you can keep it." his Dad told him.

"I'm going to find me one!" Lorne stated.

He seemed to search more intently as he walked close to the edge of the stream, now determined to find a rock specimen for himself. Finally, a stone caught his eye, and he snatched it up unceremoniously from the bed of the stream. It carried a green sheen, coupled with strands of purple and white.

"Whatcha got, Lorne?" his brother asked.

"I don't know, Taylor, but it sure is pretty!" Lorne exclaimed excitedly.

The men caught up to them, and Lorne showed his stone to them. All three admired it.

None of them had any idea what it was other than, as Lorne had stated, "It sure is pretty!"

"We better go over and check out that wooded area while we're here," Chance commented. "Maybe the one we're looking for will be among them."

They all stepped across the stream and walked toward the trees.

A few yards into the trees, the land began a gradual slope upward. It went on for nearly half a mile before it leveled out again, and then dipped down into a breathtaking arroyo that at an earlier time in history had ran rampant with water, leaving rocks of all sizes and shapes in its wake before it had finally ran dry. The bottom was now a mixture of brush, weeds, and different types of wild grasses, except where a dry riverbed channeled through the floor of it. They could see where the wildlife had made trails through the area, mapping their comings and goings.

Woody whistled. "Wow! If you boys were intending to go rock hunting, this would be the place to do it!"

His brothers agreed with him. They stood in awe of this arroyo, as if afraid to disturb the beauty before them that ran slightly to the west of where they were now standing.

After several moments, their wits came back to them, and Curtis said, "Let's walk a ways and see what we have here. We can't stay long, but we have a little time yet before we need to turn back toward the cabin."

What the boys found were pocketsful of small rocks to carry back to the cabin with them. What Chance found was a small buck deer in the sights of his rifle. And what Woody found was that his new bowie was much better at skinning the hide from it than his old knife had been on the first deer and the ram. Curtis helped his brothers skin out this deer and quarter it. He had fortunately thought to stuff some plastic bags in his coat pocket for just such an occasion.

He knew they had a sufficient supply of meat at the processing plant in town already, and with this deer in the freezer locker as well, it would hold them over until spring easily. Perhaps they could spare some for the less fortunate.

One more time, Curtis swung the fresh meat on top of the roof to freeze over night. His brother Chance picked up his new hammer and a handful of nails and stretched the first deer hide along the outside of the cabin. He did the same for the ram hide. His nephews, in spite of their excitement over their new rock collection, watched him hang the hides. He explained the procedure of hanging the hides to them as he worked. When he was through with that, he took the hammer and spare nails inside and brought back his scrapers, one of which he handed to his brother Woody.

"Take your pick, Woody," he told his brother.

Woody was nearer to the ram hide, so he began working on it.

"Why do you have to scrap the hides?" Lorne asked.

"So we can salt them down and soften them. The salt helps preserve them. If they aren't scraped, they begin to smell and rot from the degrading sinus left on the hide," Chance explained.

"And," Woody continued his brother's explanation, "we can sell the hides later. Maybe the antlers too. This year, we didn't set any traps for wildlife. In fact, we didn't buy any traps. But next year, we may want to get some and try to catch some smaller game for their hides. We don't know yet what sort of game live here. By next year, we will know and know whether or not it will be worth our time to buy traps."

"If you do decide to buy traps next year, would you teach me and Lorne how to set them?" Taylor asked.

Chance and Woody both stopped working and looked at their nephews.

After a long moment, Chance said to them, "I'm not sure you boys are strong enough to handle the traps, but if your Dad will allow it, you can both go with us to check the traps. That is, if we elect to buy some traps. But like Woody said, we don't know yet what kind of small game are in this area yet. It may not be worth our time to buy traps."

Curtis had been listening to the exchange of conversations between his brothers and his sons. He could think of nothing to add, so he merely told them supper would be ready in about a half an hour.

He was proud that his sons had taken an interest in what was happening on the new land he and his brothers had bought. He was glad too that Chance and Woody had taken the time to teach the boys as daily activities progressed for all of them. He noticed that Taylor favored his Uncle Chance, while Lorne favored his Uncle Woody.

4

After supper, the boys both brought their rocks to the table to look at them some more. They had the rocks they picked out of the stream and the ones from the arroyo.

"Can we go back to that rocky place again tomorrow?" Taylor asked his dad.

"We still have to go to the west and see what's out that way," Curtis reminded his son.

"I know, Dad, but we got two more days. Can't we go back there tomorrow and then take the west trail the next day?" Taylor asked.

Lorne was also looking hopeful.

Curtis Demming studied his sons for a few minutes. At length, he agreed with Taylor. He knew they were overran with excitement of having found the stones in the stream and also with the promise of more finds among the rocks that littered the arroyo.

"I need to take that buck to the Meat Processing Plant in the morning. I can pick up some buckets for you to put your rocks in," he told them.

They both clapped their hands and shouted, "Yeah!"

"Doesn't take much to get them excited," Chance commented.

"But you have to admit, Chance, that arroyo is gorgeous. And it probably holds a wealth of treasures for our nephews," Woody told him.

Chance smiled, recalling days long gone that he and his two brothers had searched for arrowheads and fossils, and each of them still had a handful of those treasures. They had been just as excited as his nephews were now over their rock collections.

"Seems like a long time ago that we three hunted treasures," he said to Woody.

Curtis stood by the table, watching his sons pick up each stone in turn and inspect it. Now and then, one of them would hold out his hand with "Look!" to show the others what he had found. They had some unusual stones among what they had picked up that afternoon, and he smiled as he watched the boys check each one of them over and over—treasures they'd keep for years to come.

"Want some coffee?" Woody asked him.

He took a cup and joined Woody and Chance to sit on the floor along the wall of the cabin.

"Did you guys get through with the hides?" Curtis asked them.

"We're through with the two we were working on," Chance answered. "I'll do the buck skin tomorrow while you take the meat to the Processing Plant. And unless you're taking the kids with you, I may let them scrap that hide. They need to learn how to do that, and that skin is small enough it won't matter much if they mess up."

"Sounds like a plan," Curtis replied.

Woody nodded in agreement.

"What can we do with our rocks?" Lorne asked.

"Put them in a neat little pile on the floor at the head of your cots for now," Curtis told him.

They did as he told them and then went to bed, tired but happy.

* * * * *

Curtis dropped the deer meat at the Processing Plant, and on his way back, he drove to his house to see his wife for a few minutes.

He told her what all they had been doing, then asked, "Megan, would you like to go back with me? We're going back to that arroyo when I get back, and it is an awesome place."

"Why yes, I'd love to go! Are you sure your brothers won't mind?"

"You're their favorite sister-in-law. I don't think they'd mind at all. If they do, they can get over it. Get your things. We still need to go by the Mercantile and pick up some small buckets for the boys to collect their rocks in and carry them back to the cabin."

Megan changed into a pair of jeans and a flannel shirt and found her trail shoes. She then got her jacket and her purse.

"I think I'm ready," she said, following her husband out to their pickup.

At the Mercantile, Curtis picked up two small galvanized buckets for his sons to use on their rock hunting adventure. He also bought some cookies, more juice, and some sodas. Megan picked out candy bars and chips for all of them.

"Is that all we need?" she asked Curtis.

"This should do it for now," he told her.

* * * * *

Back at the cabin, he raised his voice and said, "Look what I found!"

They looked up in surprise, then both boys ran to their mom and threw their arms around her with "Mom!" and hugged her. She hugged them back. Chance and Woody also came forward and gave her a hug.

"What are you doing out here, Mom?" Taylor ask her.

"Your dad thought I should go with you this afternoon and see that beautiful arroyo he has been telling me about," she explained.

"Oh, good! You'll love it, Mom!" Lorne told her.

"I'm sure I will, Lorne," she said. "Can I see the inside of the cabin now?"

Curtis opened the door for her, and Woody picked up the package from the back seat of the pickup. Chance carried in the juice and sodas.

Megan wasn't sure what to expect of the inside of the cabin. It totally surprised her. It was well made and roomy, and the men had kept it clean. Plus, it was warm. It not only had the fireplace but an open-faced woodstove and a cookstove. And for want of electricity and a refrigerator, the coolers sufficed to keep things cool.

"What did you use for a freezer to keep the meat frozen until you could take it to town?" she asked.

"That genius husband of yours threw it on top of the roof," Chance told her with a smile.

Looking at him, Megan asked, "Weren't you afraid of predators getting it?"

"The bears have already hibernated, and the mountain cats and wolves aren't likely to jump that high, especially in snow and dense fog," Woody told her. "So far, our meat wasn't bothered. We saved the hides. Chance and I cleaned two of them yesterday, and he showed the boys how to scrap them and salt the other one this morning."

"My goodness. You guys have been busy," she responded.

"Are you guys about ready to go rock hunting again?" Curtis asked.

He gave his sons the buckets he had bought for them in which to collect rocks, and both thanked him with excitement in their voices. They were all ready to leave, so he led the way with his wife beside him where walking would permit. Taylor and Lorne walked behind them, carrying their new buckets. Chance and Woody followed the boys.

As they reached the arroyo, Curtis told his wife, "Be careful, honey, because some of these rocks are still wet and slippery. You boys be careful too."

Megan and the boys all assured him they would be careful. Megan was awestruck at the beauty of it. She looked along it as far as she could see. It was not a surprise that her sons wanted to come back to it or that her husband wanted her to see it.

The boys clambered ahead down the trail left by wildlife, gathering numerous rocks as they went. Megan and the men walked more slowly. Curtis helped her over a couple of the rock formations as they went.

He had just helped her over the second formation when they heard a muffled yell from Lorne. Curtis hurried to where Lorne lay at the bottom of the incline he had slid down.

Taking ahold of his son, he asked, "Lorne, what happened?"

"I put my foot on a rock, and when I went to lift the other leg, the rock gave away with me," Lorne explained.

Lorne didn't seem to be hurt, just shaken.

"Stand up and let's see if either of your legs are broken," Curtis told him, holding onto Lorne's arm to help him up. His legs seemed to be okay. "Do you hurt anywhere else?"

Chance was there, and Woody was helping Megan to them. Taylor was just a few feet away.

"You okay, Lorne?" Taylor asked as he closed the gap.

"I think so," Lorne told his brother.

"I'll help you pick up your rocks – the ones that fell out of your bucket," Taylor offered.

"Cool. Thanks, Taylor," Lorne responded.

His Mother hugged him and kissed him on the forehead.

"Okay, sport, finish your rock hunting. Maybe you won't have any more mishaps," his dad told him.

"It's so beautiful out here," Megan breathed. "It makes a person just want to stay here forever."

The menfolk laughed at her but appreciated her comment. They had felt the same way yesterday. But they didn't remind her it belonged to the three of them now.

"We'd best be following those youngsters in case one or the other takes a tumble again," Woody reminded them.

The snow had melted some in places, and the boys took advantage of every bared spot to search for their treasured rocks.

Excitedly they exclaimed along the way, "There's one!"

They were enjoying the afternoon in pre-teen fashion. Only twice did the adults hear "I saw that one first!" and that was quickly resolved by one of them finding another precious stone nearby.

"I'm glad the boys are enjoying this trip so much," Megan said.

"They're certainly collecting memories," her husband responded.

"Isn't that the purpose of having a few days of vacation from school?" Chance asked.

His nephews reminded him of himself and his brothers when they were that age.

5

"Oh, look!" Megan exclaimed as she watched a mountain goat skitter across the arroyo not far from where she stood.

It ran a couple hundred yards before scrambling up the side of the arroyo. Chance could have shot it, but he figured they had enough meat already to last them through the winter. Curtis smiled at him knowingly. Chance would not shoot just for sport. He and his brothers had been brought up to know better than that.

Woody looked at Chance but said nothing, even though he silently said to himself, "Good boy, Chance."

They walked onward to where Taylor and Lorne were still searching for rocks to take back with them.

The men looked around as they walked. There were a few scattered trees along the arroyo, and it looked to be a front for a denser stand of blue spruce just to the west of it. Curtis drew his brothers' attention to it.

"We may have to come back later and check out that bunch of trees," he told them. "That may be where we find the one we are looking for."

Both brothers agreed with him.

"Why are you looking for a tree?" Megan asked.

"Because we want to find a special tree to cut and put up at home for the boys for Christmas this year," Curtis answered.

"Oh, I had no idea you guys had that in mind. I just thought you wanted to explore this new land you bought," Megan told him.

"We did. But we also thought we might find a special tree to put up for Christmas," Curtis smiled. "A live tree for them to decorate. Maybe one that will add its pine scent to the house as well."

"We still have to explore the west trail," Woody told her. "If we don't find a tree on that trail, we may come back and check these out. Meantime, my nephews are having the time of their lives out here."

"We may have to start bringing them out on the weekends when the weather permits," Chance added.

Curtis noticed neither of his brothers had ask him or Megan about bringing the boys out here on the weekends when the weather was where they could. They just assumed it would be okay. He knew they meant no disrespect either to Megan or to himself. And he knew they would look after the boys. Still, Curtis thought it would be nice if once in a while they would ask him and Megan or at least say "if your parents don't mind."

Sometimes, he wished he and his brothers weren't so close. Times like now when he felt they should have asked him or Megan about bringing the boys out here on the weekends when they could. Other times, he was glad they were close.

He looked at his watch. It was nearly four o'clock already. They needed to be getting back to the cabin.

He called to Taylor and Lorne, then asked his brothers, "Who's fixing supper tonight?"

"I guess it's about my turn since you and Woody have been doing all of it until now," Chance spoke up. "It wouldn't be fair to ask Megan to cook since this is her first night to be with us."

"I wouldn't mind cooking supper," his sister-in-law told him.

"I know you wouldn't mind," Chance said, "but you're not going to. I am and that's final."

His tone of voice told her not to argue with him. He and his brothers were all good cooks and had often helped her with the holiday cooking.

"What are you gonna cook, Uncle Chance?" Taylor asked.

"I won't know that until I look and see what all we have left," his uncle told him.

"Well, whatever it is, it'll be good," Taylor told him. "One of these times, you're gonna have to teach me and Lorne how to cook."

Chance laughed. "So I get the honor of teaching you boys how to cook, huh? Did you ever think your Mom or your Dad could teach you? And your Uncle Woody is a pretty good cook too, you know?"

"But I want *you* to teach us, Uncle Chance," Taylor insisted.

His Uncle Woody smiled knowingly. His brother Chance could outcook them all and rarely ever needed a recipe to do so. Chance had the ability to take nothing and turn it into something fantastic. He and Curtis were good cooks, but nothing to compare to Chance when he was in a mood to cook.

"I tell you what, let's let it be a family affair. You boys can learn from all of us, and you'll probably turn out to be better cooks than any of us," Chance told his nephew.

Megan laughed and said, "Probably so! But it would be a good idea for you two to learn to cook. You won't always have one of us around to do it for you."

Taylor looked from his Uncle to his Mom and said nothing more. But he was hoping she would let him start helping her in the kitchen—the sooner, the better—because he wanted to be as good a cook as his Uncle Chance. He loved his Uncle Woody, but Uncle Chance was his favorite.

6

The next morning, Curtis fixed breakfast for them, and after the dishes were washed, they set out for the western trail. It was sprinkled with trees along but not as dense as the other wooded areas. It hosted a fairly large meadow on which a small band of elk were grazing. They tried not to disturb them as they walked on westward. Here and there were small shrubs along the way, and a few birds welcomed them as they walked. To the far side of this area, they came upon what looked to be remnants of an old wagon trail road.

"What was this used for?" Lorne asked.

"I'm not sure," Curtis told his son. "It could have been a stagecoach road or it could have been a road used by miners to transport their findings to town with wagons."

"Can we check it out?" Lorne asked.

"We can walk down it a little ways and see where it goes," Curtis agreed.

"Come on, Taylor!" Lorne told his brother, as both began to run down the old road.

Curtis called to them to stop running and walk. As if he'd given a command, his brothers caught up with their nephews and walked with them. Curtis was glad. His sons would listen to their uncles, and Chance and Woody would keep an eye out for danger; whereas, the boys were young enough they didn't think about the dangers that may be lurking along that old road. He and his wife Megan followed, enjoying the walk.

"Curtis, this land you guys bought is sure pretty," Megan said.

Curtis looked at her and put an arm around her shoulders. "Maybe we'll have more time later on to enjoy it more. And by this time next year, we hope to be able to have electricity installed in the cabin."

"Oh, I don't know, Curtis. I kind of like it like it is. It gives a sense of old-time living. And the cabin is comfortable. It makes for a great getaway place," his wife remarked.

"But it would be nice to have a refrigerator, and that takes electricity," he reminded her.

"I guess you're right," she said, looking up at him with a smile. "That would allow for a TV where the boys could watch their favorite TV shows too."

"By then," he told her, "I hope they will be weaned away from some TV programs they watch and be more into sports and hunting."

"We can do the refrigerator this next year and maybe later get a TV out to the cabin," Megan suggested.

By then, their boys would be weaned from watching the TV so much. These past few days had given them some things to look forward to, and their uncles had given them the idea to look forward to coming out to the country on the weekends when the weather allowed.

Already she had seen changes in her sons. The ten-year-old and twelve year-old that she watched now were more grown-up than the ones who had left town with their dad and uncles a week ago.

Chance and Woody stopped and called their nephews back to them.

When Curtis and Megan caught up to them, Curtis asked them, "What's up?"

Chance pointed to an area some five hundred yards ahead. Curtis looked to where his brother was pointing. Ahead of them was the remnants of what looked to be an old Indian burial ground—a sacred area that they would have to respect. However, the boys wanted to go to it and rummage for treasures, a natural intrigue for young boys.

Taylor asked if they could go look for treasures. He and Lorne could spend a while going through those old piles of stones, he thought. He was excited, and he knew Lorne was excited too.

"No. Taylor and Lorne, you are *not, at any time*, to ever go to those graves. Furthermore, I don't want to hear of you bothering them in any way. If those are actual Indian burial graves. They are sacred to the Indians. And you are not to bother them. Do you understand me?" Curtis said sternly.

They both answered *yes*, but he could tell that neither of them understood why they were not allowed to look through the rocks on the graves for treasures. He could see the disappointment in their young faces.

"We should probably build some kind of fence around that burial ground," Curtis told his brothers.

They both agreed with him. They would need to find a weekend they could get away from Taylor and Lorne. The boys would be in the way. And as boys sometimes do, they would more than likely try to sneak a few "treasures" from the graves to stem their curiosity, not realizing the wrong in it or that what they would take from the graves would be stealing. Neither did they understand *why* the burial ground was sacred. They were baffled by having been told the rock piles were sacred and that they were not allowed to collect treasures that so wantonly beckoned them. After all, to the youngsters, they were just a bunch of piled-up rocks and rocks were what they were collecting.

"I wonder why the people we bought this land from didn't mention this burial ground to us," Curtis voiced his question to his brothers.

"I don't know," Chance answered him. "Could be they didn't know it was here. Or if they did, maybe they didn't know what it was other than just a few mounds of piled-up rocks."

"We'll have to report it to the Sheriff," Woody commented. "And depending on what he says about it, we may have to sign this small area back over to the State."

"Do you have to tell 'em?" Taylor asked.

"Yes, son," Curtis answered. "We don't necessarily have to do it today. We can do it the first of the week."

He added the last because he was afraid his boys might talk about the burial rock mounds at school or with their other friends.

"I'll see if I can get ahold of the County offices," Woody offered. "I may have to make a trip to Denver to the State offices though. But I'll see what I can find out."

"The State Office of Archaeology should be able to advise you on what we need to do about that Indian burial area, if it is actually an Indian burial ground. They may need to have it surveyed before they can record it," Chance told his brother. "I'm sure they will have to send reports to the State, and we may have to fill out some forms for them also."

"I'm sure we will," Curtis commented. "I doubt if we have anything to worry about where we didn't know it was there until today. At least I hope not. But it does need to be reported."

An eagle flew close overhead, screaming at them in its flight, as if to tell them they were trespassing on its domain.

"We need to make a note of the date, the time of day, and the location of this find," Megan suggested. "You may also need the legals of the land."

Her husband checked the time on his watch. "We probably need to do that as soon as we get back to the cabin. But first, Chance and Woody and I need to walk around this burial ground and get an estimated size of it. Boys, you stay here with your mother."

He and his brothers walked around the area of the burial ground, measuring each side by counting their strides as three feet. They measured 35 steps on two sides and 45 steps on the other two sides, making it one 105 feet on two sides by 135 feet on the other two sides. Most of the graves they noted had been untouched by treasure hunters, and for that, they were glad.

"How do you know those piles of rocks are Indian burial grounds?" Lorne asked.

He didn't see anything special about them. To him, they were just piles of rocks.

"His Uncle Chance stopped, looked at his nephew with a concerned look, and answered him, "I don't, but I know those should be Indian graves because of the types of stones that are laid on them and the size of the graves. If you two boys will take a few minutes to look, you will see that most of the stones at the bottoms are large stones. They have selected other stones stacked on top of the larger bottom ones creating a mound. Some of the Indians did that to keep predators from digging up their loved ones.

"Indian gravesites are sacred, much like the white man's cemeteries, and they are not to be bothered, just as the white man's cemeteries are not to be bothered. And if they are not Indian graves, they may go back to some prehistoric time. Either way, they are not to be disturbed. Do you boys have any more questions?"

Their uncle's explanation seemed to satisfy their curiosity, and both shook their heads no.

Lorne looked at his uncle and commented, "Uncle Chance, you sure are smart."

Chance smiled at his nephew, put an arm around his shoulders, and told him, "When you get as old as I am, maybe you'll be as smart as I am or maybe smarter."

They returned to where Megan waited. Their Uncle Chance, their Dad, and Uncle Woody walked the rest of the way back to the cabin with them and their mother.

* * * * *

Back at the cabin, Taylor asked, "What kind of Indians lived here in the old days?"

"The ones that came and went through this area were the Utes, the Navajos, the Jicarilla Apaches, the Crow, some of the Comanches and Cherokees, and probably some other tribes as well," his Dad answered.

"Well then, what Indian tribe would those graves belong to?" Taylor wanted to know.

"It's hard to say, son," Curtis said. "It would depend on which tribe had settled there and maybe even how long they had stayed. Indians moved about with the seasons, just as the animals migrate to different areas during the spring and fall. Many of them followed the buffalo so they could kill them for meat for their families and hides to use for building their teepees, for clothing and bedding, and, at times, for trading at the Indian trading posts for other provisions."

"There's lots of history associated with this area," Uncle Woody put in. "There were not only Indians but also French and later Germans. There were also Spanish and Europeans before the American people came."

"Wow!" his nephews exclaimed almost in unison.

Uncle Woody had caught their attention. Now their young minds could comprehend more of what Uncle Chance had told them, their interests grew. To them, Uncle Woody was as smart as Uncle Chance. The beginning of understanding grew inside of them.

Megan who had sat quietly at the table listening now stated, "I didn't know about any of this. I guess I better see what else me and the boys can find out."

Chance had been fixing their evening meal and now began to set the table. His sister-in-law helped him. Soon they were all enjoying the feast Chance had prepared.

"You know," Megan interrupted their eating, "it might be a good idea for us to bring the camera with us next time and get pictures of that burial ground."

7

Woody was up first the next morning. He added more wood to the fireplace and then to the wood burning stove. Afterward he checked for what he could fix them for breakfast. Looked like they were going to have bacon and eggs with some pan-fried toast. He set the items on the counter then commenced to make a pot of coffee.

They would check along the west trail again that day. They started with the south trail, went east, and then later north. After Curtis brought Megan out, they went north again. Yesterday they went west where they found the old road and the Indian burial ground. Today would be their last day together for a while. He and his brothers had to go back to work and the boys back to school.

"I smell coffee and bacon," Curtis said, coming into the kitchen.

Chance had also gotten up. They poured coffee and sat drinking it, letting Megan and the boys sleep.

Finally Curtis, broke the silence by asking, "Didn't there use to be a coal mine somewhere out in this area?"

"I don't know," Chance answered. "I've heard tales of gold strikes near the mountains, but I haven't heard any rumors about a coal mine."

"You're behind on your history, Chance," Woody said. "There was a fellow named Fred Walsen who found and operated the first coal mine out here. It's said the coal mining produced over five hundred million tons of coal. He also built and operated a large Mercantile that catered to the German settlers. And he also helped build the town, which was later named for him and became Walsenburg."

"You think we might find some coal on this place?" Taylor wanted to know.

They all smiled at him.

His dad answered, "Probably not enough to brag about. But it's possible there may be a few small chunks lying around somewhere that you boys could add to your rock collections."

"I hope so," Lorne said. "That would be cool to have our own piece of coal."

"It may be a while before we find any," Curtis told them. "So don't get your hopes up too high."

"Yeah, but, Dad, there's still a lot places we haven't been to yet," Taylor reminded him. "And it would be cool to find some coal somewhere."

Curtis smiled and conceded that it might be cool at that. At least it gave his boys something to look forward to.

Woody made coffee and now he poured the four adults each a cup.

"Breakfast will be ready in a few minutes," he told them.

The boys set their buckets of rocks next to their beds and would put the earlier collected rocks in with today's finds. These would go home with them to be proudly shown to their friends later on.

Chance made sure his knives and scrapers were cleaned, oiled, and put away and his rifle cleaned and oiled as well. He would leave them there at the cabin so they would be there when he and his brothers were able to come back.

Megan now set the table and began to help Woody set the food on it.

"You boys get washed for breakfast," she said.

Her sons beat her husband and her brothers-in-law to the table. While Megan ate, she noticed the men and boys ate with a zest they had not had with their meals in town. They ate more all the while teeming with excitement of exploring the west trail again that day.

She felt her own excitement rising, and immediately after the dishes were done, all of them were into coats, hats, and gloves and raring to go.

The southernmost side of the western trail proved to be the area most visited by the resident wildlife. Here they found more elk, deer, and antelope that gathered to graze the lush grass. Rabbits were also inhabitants of this area, and more birds lived in this area also. The wildlife mostly raised their heads to look at the humans and went back to feeding. The birds chattered their welcome chirps and flew to tree limbs or ground areas where they fed on insects, berries, and grass seeds. Trees in the area were abundant too and seemed to outline the meadow in which the wildlife grazed.

The sky had cleared to a beautiful shade of blue with only a few drifting clouds overhead. The few Aspen trees amid the other trees gave the fall colors a touch of beauty. Far to the western slope was a wall of jagged boulders that gave limited protection from the cold winter winds.

"This would make a good hay meadow," Curtis commented. "We could cut it and bale what we need, and there would still be enough left for the wildlife."

"Why would we want to do that?" Chance asked.

"Because we could sell the hay or maybe buy a few head of horses or donkeys to train and sell," Curtis told him.

"Curtis, I haven't trained a horse in years," Chance told him.

"And neither have I," Woody added.

"I have to admit, I haven't either. But Dad taught us all how to do it when we were younger. And if we just get a few, like two or three to start with, it wouldn't take it long for what we learned from Dad to come back to us, and it just might mean some extra income for us. At least we can think on it," Curtis told them.

"Boy, when you come up with an idea, you make work for all of us," Chance mused out loud with a smile.

He liked his brother's idea though, but it would be tough. With all three of them working regular jobs, it wasn't often they had several days off together like they did this week.

Woody agreed with Chance. It had been a long time since he had ridden a horse, much less trained one. And he couldn't remember ever training a donkey. Yet he knew there were still people who even that day worked mines out this way, and it was possible that some of them did still use donkeys.

They would need to buy posts and wood to build the corral and a round pen in which they could train the animals. He studied the area around him, and a visual image came to him as to where and how to transform the layout. He pointed to a place near the edge of the meadow close to where they now stood and related his vision to his brothers.

"We could build a large corral right there," he extended his right arm and pointed to where he was talking about. "We could build a round pen a few feet from it. We can also build a shed for them."

"And," Chance added, "we can also build a shed and a holding pen near the cabin where we can bring in the trained animals to show to customers."

Curtis agreed with them both.

8

The next morning while everyone else was gathering their things, Curtis pulled his truck forward and loaded the deer meat into the bed. After that, he went back inside the cabin. "Is everyone ready to go?" he asked.

His brothers had only the clothes they had been wearing the past several days. The boys had their soiled clothes and their rock collections. His wife had only the clothes she had originally worn and her purse. Woody sat in the back with his nephews, and Megan sat between Chance and her husband.

Curtis headed his truck toward his house. They unloaded everything but the deer meat. Chance and Woody took their belongings to their own vehicles while Megan and the boys carried their things inside the house.

"I'll be back in a couple of hours," Curtis told them. "I'm going to run this deer meat to the Packing Plant."

"We'll stay and help Megan with whatever she needs for tomorrow's dinner," Chance told him. "You should be back in time for the football game. This one should be a good game. It's between the 49ers and the Dallas Cowboys."

"I should be back in plenty of time for that," Curtis commented.

It wasn't quite noon when Curtis pulled up in front of the Meat Processing Plant.

He got the bag of deer meat out of his truck and carried it inside.

The clerk met him with a smile. "Looks like you guys are going to have a good winter."

"I hope so," Curtis told him. "If you know of anyone needing this buck . . . like a nursing home or food bank or anyone else in need, you can give this one to them."

"Thank you, Mr. Demming. I do happen to know of a family that can well use this meat. I'll see that they get it," the clerk said.

Curtis nodded and said, "Thanks. You have a good Thanksgiving."

Back at his house, he told his wife and brothers what he had told the clerk at the Meat Processing Plant.

"Curtis, that was a wonderful thing to do," Megan told him.

"Between now and Christmas, maybe we can bring in another deer or two," Chance offered.

"We better do it sometime this week, Chance. Deer season is about over," Woody reminded his brother.

"I hadn't thought of that," Chance admitted.

"We can go back out tomorrow and see what we can come up with," Curtis suggested. "For that matter, we have time this evening to go back out and see what we can come up with."

"I thought you wanted to watch the football game?" Woody said.

"Put it on record. We can watch it tomorrow while we enjoy Thanksgiving dinner," Curtis told him.

"What will you do with the meat, Curtis?" Megan asked him.

"We have the coolers now that we can put it in. Or if need be, I can put it on top of the cabin like we've been doing," her husband replied. "There are people who need to eat worse than we need to sit in front of a TV."

"Dad, can we go with you?" Taylor asked.

"No, Taylor. You and Lorne see what you can do to help your mother, okay?"

He saw the disappointment on Taylor's face and on Lorne's too. But they were young, and they would soon get over it. He was confident their mother could find things for them to do while he and their uncles were on their quest for finding meat for the local needy people. His sons didn't realize that Curtis and his brothers were disappointed too at having to record the football game they had all fervently wanted to watch.

"I hope you have a lot of good luck," Megan told him, giving him a hug and a kiss. "I'll have supper ready by the time you get home."

He smiled at her. "I love you, Megan."

He turned from her and joined his brothers at his truck for the trip back to the cabin.

Looking at his gas gauge he said, "We better find a service station before we wish we had and fill this old boy up."

"I'll pay for the gas," Woody volunteered.

The station Curtis stopped at had a Mini-Mart. They each bought sandwiches and snacks to tide them over until they got back from hunting.

At the cabin, Chance started a small fire in the fireplace to take the chill from the rooms.

Getting his rifle and skinning knife, he suggested, "Guys, let's take Trail Number Four and see if we can come up on that herd of elk again. One large elk would feed quite a few people."

Woody and Curtis both collected their skinning knives. Curtis also gathered several plastic bags to put the meat in. It would take at least a couple of trips back to the cabin to carry the meat and the hide and antlers. That is, of course, if they were to get an elk. And he hoped they did. Excitement began to rise in all three of them as they left the cabin and walked westward toward the meadow where they had seen the elk the day before.

When they reached the meadow, the elk were grazing toward the tree line to the southwest of them. They counted seventeen. They walked slowly around the easterly side of the meadow and followed its boundary at the south end westward toward the elk.

They were well within shooting range of Chance's rifle when one of the elk raised its head to look in their direction. The men stopped and stood motionless so as not to spook their quarry. Chance dropped to one knee and put the rifle site on a large elk. He waited a few minutes before he fired. The elk stumbled a few feet, spooking the others, and fell onto the lush grass of the meadow.

Chance rose, and his brothers followed him to where the elk lay. They admired it openly. It was a beautiful bull elk. It had fallen in such a way as to not break any of the points on his antlers.

"Lucky!" exclaimed Chance. That rack would look nice mounted and hung on the wall.

"Let's see if we can find a couple of poles that we can carry him back to the cabin on,' Curtis suggested.

He wasn't sure how well the plastic bags he had brought along would work, but he figured if they put one bag inside another and cut holes in the bottoms to push the poles through, they could roll the elk onto the bags and thus create a type of carrying sling to take him to the cabin.

Woody helped him get the poles through the bags. They would have to hoist the poles on to their shoulders in order to carry the elk back to the cabin without dragging and possibly breaking the rack. Chance helped his brothers get the elk in place on the bags and then helped them lift the poles to their shoulders.

Long before they reached the cabin, both Curtis and Woody were aching through their arms and shoulders.

"We're going to have to make a road to that meadow," Curtis said. "That way, I can bring the truck next time we need to carry something home."

His brothers agreed with him. But at last they reached Curtis's truck where Chance directed the loading of the elk from the shoulders of his two brothers into the bed of the truck, careful not to break the rack.

Woody went inside the cabin to make sure the fireplace had burned down to a safe level of glowing coals. Rejoining his brothers told them he was ready to go back to town.

Chance had put the safety on his rifle so it wouldn't accidently fire and lay it on the back seat beside him. He would clean it later. Right now, he knew they needed to get the elk to the Meat Processing Plant. They wouldn't have much time to spare when they got there as it was.

Curtis explained the elk to the clerk and apologized for not having taken the time to field dress it before they brought it in.

"But I wanted to get it here before you closed. We'd like to keep the antler rack, but the rest is for the needy people."

"Pull around back, and we'll get it unloaded," the clerk told him.

Curtis pulled his truck around into the alley behind the Meat Processing Plant and backed it as close as he dared to the plant door. The clerk came outside with a small cable that he attached to the back legs just above the hooves. He attached a large hook to the cable between the legs and began slowly winching the elk from the back of Curtis Demming's truck. Chance and Woody helped guide the carcass as the winch pulled it slowly into a hanging position inside the plant. The clerk hoisted it high enough so that the antler rack did not touch the floor.

"Thank you, Mr. Demming. I still have about an hour before I close, but I can work as long as I need to on this elk after I close. I'll put a couple of roasts from it into your locker so your family can enjoy part of what you have so generously donated to the hungry in our area," the clerk responded. "I will call you one day next week to pick up the rack."

"Thanks, and Happy Thanksgiving to you and your family," Curtis told the clerk as he headed for the door of the shop.

"Wait! I forgot to ask if you want the hide," the clerk stated.

The Demming men looked at each other without answering.

So the clerk continued, "If you don't care to have it, I know of a Mexican family just outside of town who could use it. They are very poor, and this hide would be good to serve as a rug for the floor of their small house and would keep the children from having to walk on the cold dirt floor in bare feet."

Again, the brothers looked at each other. Woody broke the silence.

"How long did you say you'd be open?"

"For about another hour, sir," the clerk told him.

"Don't lock the front door until we get back," Woody told him.

The clerk was puzzled but told Woody, "Okay."

They unloaded the poles with the garbage bags from the truck, then found a grocery store just a few blocks away. They filled a shopping cart with a variety of canned vegetables, seasonings, juices, and other things they thought the Mexican family might be in need of, including milk and eggs. They paid at the register and carried the sacks of groceries to the truck and returned to the Meat Processing Plant.

Curtis knocked on the door and entered the building. The clerk greeted him and looked immediately surprised as Chance and Woody deposited sacks filled with groceries on the floor.

"What's that for?" he asked them.

"That's for the needy Mexican family you told us about," Chance answered him.

"Go ahead and take them some of that deer meat too. You can process the elk later. And tell them Happy Holidays for us."

9

It was getting dark when Curtis stopped his truck in his driveway. He and his brothers entered the house where the smell of the supper Megan had fixed met them.

"I kept your supper warm for you. How did your afternoon go?" Megan asked.

"It went okay, Megan. We went back on Trail Number Four—you remember where we saw the elk the other day?—and a large bull elk with a beautiful antler rack walked in front of Chance's rifle. We had to rig a sling with a couple of poles and some of the garbage bags. Then me and Woody carried him back to the truck. It took all three of us to load him without damaging his rack. But we managed. Then we took him to Pueblo to the Meat Packing Plant. When we got there, the clerk had me drive around to the back of his shop to unload him. He put a length of cable around his back legs and a big hook and hoisted him out of the truck bed. Woody and Chance helped keep the rack from getting damaged. We told the clerk we wanted the rack," Curtis informed his wife, aware that his sons had come in and were standing behind their uncles listening.

"The clerk asked us if we wanted the hide," Chance continued his brother's conversation. "He said he knows a Mexican family who can use it for a rug on the floor of their small house so their kids don't have to walk barefoot on the dirt floor."

"That's awful!" Megan interrupted. "When you pick up the elk antlers, why don't you ask that clerk if he knows what size shoes those kids wear and where they live? Maybe Santa Clause could help their situation out a bit."

"That's a good idea, Megan," Chance told her. "We could have the clerk at the Meat Processing Plant show us how to get out to their place. We can introduce ourselves to the Mexican family, and who knows? If we like the husband, maybe we can let him help us later on out on our place with building the corrals and such. He might even know where we can pick up some horses and mules to train."

"We'll see. They are a very poor family. We went to the grocery store and bought them some groceries and took those back to the clerk to deliver to them. I told him to give them some of the deer meat also. He can work on the elk later," Curtis told her.

"That was good of you guys!" Megan exclaimed.

"But why do they have dirt floors?" Lorne asked.

"Because, son, they do not have the money to put regular floors in their house. It takes all the man can do to keep food on the table, and sometimes that's pretty skimpy," Curtis explained.

"How do they stay warm?" Taylor asked.

"Mostly they don't. They bundle up in layers of clothing and what blankets they have. They use mud to fill in the gaps between the boards or posts that their homes are made of to keep out the wind. They burn wood for heat. But mostly, though, they do not know warm as we know warm," Curtis told his son.

"But don't they have shoes?" Lorne wanted to know. His young mind couldn't fathom kids without shoes.

"No," Uncle Woody answered. "Their feet are sometimes wrapped in rags, but they have no shoes to wear. And believe me, cold dirt floors are not exactly what you want to walk on with bare feet, especially in the winter time."

"The clerk may be still at the shop. Let me call and see," Curtis said, getting up to go to the phone.

He took the receipt for the locker out of his wallet and dialed the number on it. It rang several times. No one answered.

"I guess he's either gone for the day or he doesn't want anyone to know he's still there working in the back," Curtis stated, putting his receipt back in his wallet.

"Well, we can try again tomorrow. I just hope he took the groceries on out to the Mexican family," Chance told him. "It bothers me to know there's people out there that are too poor to feed their families."

"Why don't they get jobs?" Taylor asked. "Are they just too lazy to work?"

"Taylor, a lot of people won't hire Mexicans just because they are a different culture. A lot of people don't trust them. A lot the Mexicans don't have proper clothes to wear, even if they could get jobs. And without decent clothes to wear, people aren't going to hire them," Chance explained to his nephew.

"That don't make sense!" Taylor exclaimed.

"Well, son, that's the way it is in today's world. To work, you have to have decent clothes that are clean every day. If you don't have proper clothes, even if you have to wash them every night after work, then you're not going to get a job. And it doesn't matter if you're Mexican, Indian, Chinese, White, or some other race," Curtis told him. "Just be thankful we have what we have and are able to help folks now and again."

"I wouldn't want to live like that," Taylor declared.

"You don't know the truth of what you just said," his Uncle Woody told him.

Woody had a faraway look in his eyes. He was remembering days of his youth when his Dad had barely been able to keep food on the table. He had taught the boys to hunt, and their mother never complained. They had not been as desperately poor as the Mexican family the clerk at the Meat Processing Plant had told them about. But they hadn't been far from it. Chance had become an excellent shot with the rifle their Dad had given him—the same one he still used. Woody could shoot but not nearly as well as Chance. He had grown up learning to use a bolo for hunting, and although he hadn't used one in years, he was pretty sure he still knew how. That was something he needed to teach his nephews.

Curtis was a decent shot with a rifle too. But while they hunted together, he let Chance have the honor of being the rifle man. As a boy, Curtis had gotten to be good with the slingshot. He used it for rabbits and squirrels. And once Woody had witnessed Curtis hitting a large rattler in the head with a stone from his slingshot. It slithered on out of sight.

But he knew his young nephews could not yet understand the depths of poverty. Curtis made sure they always had enough, even when he and Chance weren't there to help him.

"Penny for your thoughts!" Megan said to him.

"They're worth a lot more than that," Woody told her.

She laughed at him.

"Well, come on and eat. Supper's ready," she said.

10

The next morning, Curtis Demming prepared to clean out the garage to make room for adding a few shelves on which to put things. His garage was wide and also long. His truck and Megan's car fit comfortably inside with several feet to spare, both in length and width. He would need to go into Walsenburg and pick up some lumber, screws, and brackets to mount the shelves to the walls inside the garage. Not only did he want to add new shelves to allow for his tools and the holiday decorations but also to allow for Taylor and Lorne to have a place to put their rock collections and other things they valued.

Chance went home to his house a few blocks south. Woody decided to drive on to Denver and see what he could find out about where to report the burial grounds they had come up on while walking the western side of the land he and his brothers bought.

He went inside the house and asked Megan if she needed anything from town. She couldn't think of anything at the moment, so he told her he'd be back soon.

He parked in front of the Lumber Yard and went in. He didn't see anyone but figured they were either busy or shorthanded or both. He found the wall with the type of boards he wanted. He found one bin cheaper than the other bins. But after inspecting those boards, he decided against buying any of them. Some of them had slight splits in them, mostly toward the edges. He saw two with knot holes in them and several with slight warps. He went to find a cart and returned to where he had been. One of the male clerks had seen him and came to where he was standing.

"Can I help you with something?" the clerk asked him.

Curtis told the man what he needed, including brackets and screws to use with his drill.

He picked up an extra packet of the screws, just in case he would need them.

"Will there be anything else?" the clerk asked Curtis.

"I think that'll do it for this time. Thanks for your help."

At the register, he thought about some wood glue and some shellac for the boards once he got the shelves made but decided against it for now. He could get that later. He paid his bill and took his merchandise to his truck and loaded. He took the cart back inside before leaving.

He thought his boys would be catching up on the TV shows they had missed out on while out at the cabin. Instead, he found them pre-occupied with admiring their rock collections. They had spread them out on their beds and were inspecting them against a paper printout they had no doubt ran off from his or Megan's computers. He chose not to disturb them. Instead, he went into the kitchen where Megan was mixing a cake and let her know he was back.

"I'll be in the garage if you need me," he told her.

Curtis got out his drill and laid it aside with the screws he bought. Laying one board on the floor of the garage, he spaced the brackets where he thought they would do the most good and marked the boards in case the drill's vibration would cause them to jiggle out of place. He then attached the brackets one by one to that board. Next he measured down from the ceiling to where he wanted to mount that shelf to the wall. He found a ladder to be his assistant at holding the boards where he wanted them while he drilled the screws in place in the brackets at the wall. Then he stepped back to admire his work.

Satisfied he had it where it would do the most good, he picked up another board and repeated the process, placing the second shelf below the first one at fifteen inches. One more shelf found itself the same measurement from the second shelf. After that, he quit until he could decide where he wanted to put up the rest of the shelves. He laid his drill, the brackets, and the remaining screws on the last shelf.

He returned to the house and found a chair in the living room to sit down in. Then it dawned on him—he was bored. It wasn't yet four o'clock, and he had nothing to do. He would finish the garage shelves tomorrow and mow the lawn. He could finish that today, but then he would have nothing to do tomorrow. And he didn't go back to work until the day after. He turned on the TV and found a Western movie to watch.

"Honey, would you like a cup of coffee?" his wife asked.

"Yes. Thank you," he said.

She handed him a cup of coffee then sat down in the chair next to him and watched the western movie with him.

It was almost over by the time Taylor and Lorne came in to join them.

"That cake sure does smell good, Mom," Lorne told his Mom.

"I guess I better check on it," Megan said and went to the kitchen and checked on the cake.

It was ready to come out of the oven, so she took it out and set it on the burners and turned the oven off. Then she rejoined her family to watch the rest of the movie.

* * * * *

Woody didn't have a day off from the Tourist Center for three days. He elected to drive to Denver instead of looking things up on his computer. He had the notion he could get more and better information by talking directly with the clerks. His first stop was at the County Clerk's office.

"Can I help you, sir?" asked a middle-aged woman.

"I hope so," Woody told her. "I need to know where to report a burial ground on the property me and my brothers bought a few weeks ago."

"I'm sorry, sir. I don't know," she told him. "You might check with Mr. Dunhurst at the college. He teaches Archaeology classes. He might be able to give you some advice."

"Thank you, ma'am," Woody told her.

He left the Courthouse and drove to the college where he sought out Mr. Dunhurst.

The instructor introduced himself as Paul Dunhurst, Professor of Archaeology. He was a man of medium height, graying hair, and wire-rimmed glasses.

Woody introduced himself. He then explained to Paul Dunhurst about he and his brothers finding what they believed to be an old Indian burial ground on the land they had purchased a few weeks ago.

"How do we go about reporting the burial ground?" Woody asked. "What paperwork do we need to fill out?"

"Have you reported the find to your local Sheriff?" Dunhurst asked him.

"No, not yet. We thought we had to report it to an Archaeologist," Woody replied.

"You need to report it to your Sheriff first and let him and the Coroner and have them take a look at it," the instructor explained to him. "And depending on what they decide, it may be necessary to have the State Archaeologist take a thorough survey of the area. After that, he or she would need to have to make out an Archaeological report, which is about four pages long. It covers information on the Project Overview, the Project Location, the Project Area Details, a Records Review to confirm whether or not the site has ever been previously recorded, a Field Investigation, and Recommendation. These results in turn would need to be reported to the State Department of Natural Resources."

"Good Heavens! Where do I get the forms for this information?" Woody asked Mr. Dunhurst.

"You won't need them. I have some forms here I can bring with me. And I have a friend who is the local State Archaeologist for this area. I will get with him and see when he can come out to your place, Mr. Demming. I doubt very seriously that these are any tribe of Indian burial grounds, but if he can find time to come look at them, he will know more about what needs to be done," Mr. Dunhurst stated. "Let me have a phone number by which to contact you, and as soon as I can confer with my friend, I will give you a call."

The man handed Woody a piece of paper and an ink pen. Woody wrote down his name and phone number and also Chance's and Curtis's.

Handing the pen and paper back to Mr. Dunhurst, he said, "These other two are my brothers and their numbers. I will let them know I gave you their numbers also. Any one of us can show you where our land is. Just give one of us a call so we will know when to expect you."

"Thank you, Mr. Demming." Dunhurst told him.

"Thanks. And thanks for your help. I'm glad I met you. We'll be looking forward to your call," Woody said.

"My pleasure meeting you, and I am looking forward to working with you and your brothers," the Professor replied, reaching his arm out to shake hands with Woody.

Woody Demming was confident he would not have received the same information had he just called instead.

He stopped by Curtis's house enroute to his own home. He was met by his sister-in-law who bade him to come in.

"Megan, is Curtis home?" he asked her.

"No, Woody, but he should be here by six or a little before," she answered.

"Yeah, I forgot he had to go back to work too," he commented, more to himself than to her. "Would you mind if Chance and I have supper with you guys tonight?"

"Woody, you know you don't have to ask, and neither does Chance," she told him.

"Okay. I'll call Chance. How about if we get here about seven this evening?" he asked.

"That will be perfect," Megan assured him. "See you later then."

11

When he got home to his house, Woody Demming called the auto dealership where Chance worked and asked to speak to him. The employee told him "just a minute," laid the phone down, and called out for Chance to come to the phone.

Moments later, Chance answered "What's up?"

"We are going to meet at Curtis and Meg's house for supper so I can tell the rest of you what I learned today in Denver. I told Megan we'd be there about seven. Curtis gets off work at six, so that should be time for all of us to be at his house by seven," Woody explained to him.

"Sounds good, Woody. I get off in about a half an hour, hopefully. I'm with a customer at the moment, but we should be able to wrap up their deal in a few more minutes. See you at little brother's later," Chance said and hung up the phone.

He went back to his customers and apologized to them for having to interrupt their shopping.

"Oh, that's fine," the woman said. "We think we want the beige Mercury."

Chance smiled at her. "That's a nice car. You'll get good service, and I think you will be satisfied with it."

The woman and the man with her, whom Chance assumed was her husband, smiled at each other.

Then the man said, "Let's get the paperwork done."

Chance told him okay and walked with the couple to his office inside the dealership. He filled in the contract, and the man signed it, then made out a check for the total on the contract. Chance stood and shook hands with the man.

"Thank you, sir, for doing business with us," he told them.

He put the papers where they belonged, told his boss he was leaving a few minutes early to take care of some family business, and left to go home and shower before meeting Woody and Curtis at Curtis's house.

* * * * *

He arrived at his brother's house a few minutes early. His nephews greeted him at the door with hugs.

"You gonna stay for supper, Uncle Chance?" Lorne asked him.

"I thought I might," Uncle Chance told him, giving his nephews return hugs.

"Did you guys get your rock collections sorted out and labeled?"

"Not all of them, Uncle Chance. We're still trying to find out what some of them are," his nephew Taylor told him. "But I found a lot of them on the internet and a few of them in the book about rocks and minerals Dad bought us."

"Is your Dad home?" Uncle Chance asked the boys.

"Yeah. He's in the shower," Lorne answered.

"I guess that means your mom is in the kitchen. And whatever she's fixing, it smells super good."

Chance took off his jacket and laid it over the back of an easy chair and then sat down in it. Curtis joined him, taking a chair next to him. Noticing Chance didn't have anything to drink, he left and came back with a cup of coffee for each of them.

"Woody should be here shortly," Curtis told Chance. "He wanted us all together while he explains what he found out in Denver today."

"That makes sense. That way, he won't have to repeat himself. He can tell it to us once and be done with it," Chance commented.

"You have a good day at work?" Curtis asked.

"Fair," Chance told him. "I sold one car off the lot and have another being brought in from Lamar for a customer tomorrow."

They heard Megan tell Woody on his way through the door, "You're just in time to set the table!"

"Let me hang my coat and wash my hands and I'll get that done," Woody told her.

Minutes later, he was back in the kitchen setting plates and silverware while his sister-in-law put food on the table.

Once they were all seated around the table, Woody began.

"I asked Megan to invite everyone to supper tonight because I didn't want to have to repeat what I have to tell you, or forget to tell something to one or the other of you."

He paused while they passed food around the table and filled their plates.

With that done, Curtis asked him, "Well, what did you find out?"

"I had to drive out to the college and look up the instructor for Archaeology, a Mr. Paul Dunhurst. I asked him who we have to report that Indian burial ground to. He told me we will have to have to report the burial ground to the Sheriff and the Coroner, and depending on what they decide will determine whether or not we actually need to have the State Archaeologist take a look at it.

"Uncle Woody, when do you have to do that?" Taylor asked him.

"Whenever Mr. Dunhurst calls one of us, either me, Chance, or your Dad. He is a friend of the State Archaeologist. He is going to get ahold of him and then let us know when they can meet us out at the cabin. Chance and Curtis, I gave him your phone numbers too, in case I wasn't where I could answer my phone when he calls."

Curtis and Chance both told Woody that it was okay with them that he had done that.

"There are other forms we may have to fill out later too, such as the Project Location, the Project Area Details, and Records Review to find out if the site has been previously reported at some time or another. And then there is a Field Investigation and Recommendation report that has to be filled out and turned in to the State Department of Natural Resources," Woody explained to them.

"Wow! That's an awful lot of reports you guys have to fill out, Uncle Woody!" Lorne exclaimed.

His brothers started to comment too, but Woody silenced them with a raise of his right arm.

"That's not all," he said. "There are a lot of other forms the Archaeologist may have to fill out. Mr. Dunhurst has copies of those he can bring with him. And I'm pretty sure the State Archaeologist will have some also. So, guys, that concludes my findings for today."

"No wonder you wanted us all together," Chance commented. "Did the instructor give you any estimation on how soon he could let us know anything?"

"He couldn't do that, Chance, until he gets ahold of the State Archaeologist and finds out when that person is available to come out here, and he or she may want to wait until the Sheriff and the Coroner decide what to do," Woody replied.

Chance and Curtis both nodded in understanding.

"Well, Woody, you did good. Thank you for making the trip. And thank you for letting us know what you found out. I think I speak for all of us in saying we appreciate it, brother."

12

It was Saturday when Curtis answered the phone to find Chance on the other end of it.

"What's up, Chance?" Curtis asked, hoping Chance had heard something from the College Professor or could tell him Woody had heard from him.

"I only had to work half a day today. I thought if you're not too busy, we might want to build a bridge across that stream so we can get our Christmas tree home when we find it. And also so we can show the Archaeology people where that Indian burial ground is," Chance suggested.

"Sounds like a plan. Let me get my tools and I'll meet you at the Lumber Yard," Curtis agreed.

At the Lumber Yard, they bought the wood, railroad ties, and screwnails they would need to build the bridge for crossing the stream. Curtis thought to have the man cut them to save him and Chance some extra time at the stream.

Back at the cabin, Curtis made a trip to the outhouse before they drove Trail Number Three to the stream. Chance took the lead with his vehicle to mark the road they would also clear next time he and Curtis, or he and Woody, or all three had time they could apply to doing that.

Curtis turned his truck to where the wood and his tools in his truck were easily accessible. Chance did the same with his pickup. He hauled the railroad ties and his tools in his pickup. They laid the railroad ties across the stream and used one of the boards to measure how far apart they wanted the ties. After doing that, Chance dug four-inch trenches on both sides of the stream to lay the ends of the ties in. Curtis helped him lay the ties across. Afterward, it didn't take long for them lay the two-by-six boards across the ties and apply the screwnails. Their new bridge proudly spanned the stream and extended three feet to either side of it.

Curtis and Chance admired their handiwork for a few minutes.

"That ought to hold anything we can put across it," Chance commented.

"Let's give it a try," Curtis said and got into his truck, turned it around, and drove across the new bridge with his brother Chance a few feet behind in his pickup. They honked at each other, smiled, and gave a thumbs-up sign to each other before driving back across the new bridge and heading home.

* * * * *

Megan and the boys met Curtis as he stepped out of his truck at their house.

She and his sons both wanted to know, asking, "Where've you been?"

He grinned at them and gave each of them a hug before answering.

"Me and Chance built a bridge over that small stream out on Trail Number Three. And now we can drive across that side of the land and not have to walk it."

"Didn't Woody go with you?" Megan asked.

"No. Woody had to work today. Chance only worked until noon, and I had the day off," Curtis told her. "The first time we get a chance, we will clear a road through from the cabin to the meadows. Woody may be able to help with that, but at least Chance and I got a bridge built across the stream. That'll make it easier on all of us to get to where we need to go."

"I guess you didn't have time to look for a tree then," Megan commented.

"No. We just built the bridge and decided to get in out of this cold," he said, opening the door to the house for all of them.

He followed them in, removed his coat, and sat down in the living room. Megan brought him a cup of coffee, which he greatly appreciated.

"I think," he said, "both Chance and Woody are off this coming Tuesday. I am too. So we'll go find a tree and get it home so you and the boys can get it decorated before Christmas gets here without it."

The phone rang, and Curtis answered it. It was the man from the Meat Processing Plant.

"Mr. Demming, this is Ron Belcher from the Meat Processing Plant in Pueblo. I wanted to let you know your elk antler rack is ready for pickup whenever you want to come get it," he told Curtis.

"Did you take the groceries to that Mexican family you told us about?" Curtis asked him.

"Yes I did. And they are ever so grateful to you for them. I have the hide almost finished, then I will take that out to them also," Belcher told him.

"I keep forgetting to ask you . . . what is that Mexican man's name?" Curtis asked.

"His name is Juan Diego," Belcher replied. "His wife is Lucila. The kids are named Luis, Manuela, and Mateo."

"Would you say he is trustworthy?" Curtis wanted to know.

"Well, sir, he's honest. Just poor. And has a hard time keeping his family fed," the Mr. Belcher told him.

"I'd like to meet him sometime. My brothers and I may have some work we could use him for later on. And my wife wants to know what sizes they wear in clothes and shoes," Curtis told him.

"Could you meet me at the Plant this Sunday and follow me to his place?" Belcher asked.

"We'll be there," Curtis agreed.

"Thanks, Mr. Demming. I'll see you Sunday then," Belcher commented and hung up the phone.

"Megan, that was the man from the Meat Processing Plant over in Pueblo. He has the antler rack ready. I asked him about that Mexican family. He said to meet him at the Plant this Sunday and follow him out there. I'll call Chance and Woody. They can come in one of their vehicles. I think once we meet that family, we will know more how to help them, if they will let us. Some families are too proud to accept help. I hope this guy isn't that way," Curtis told her.

"I hope not too, Curtis," she answered.

Megan loved children, and the thought of those little Mexican children not having shoes or even warm-enough clothes didn't set well with her. And Curtis was right. Once she saw them, she would know more about what sizes they wore and also what sizes the parents wore. She knew Walsenburg had a Thrift store. Their prices were reasonable. She could pick up some articles there. Maybe even some cookware for the woman if she needed them. Not every place accepted Mexicans or Indians, but Megan could shop there any time. And if people got nosey, she would just tell them she was shopping for some of her family. They probably wouldn't know the difference, and it was none of their business why she bought the things she would buy in their store. She would look in her closet also and see if she didn't have an extra blanket or two she could take them. By Sunday, she would have cookies baked that she would take to the Mexican family.

Her husband called his brothers and told them what Mr. Belcher had just told him.

They both agreed to meet him at the Meat Processing Plant in Pueblo on Sunday to follow Belcher out to where the Mexican family lived. They, too, were anxious to meet the Mexican family and take stock of the man. They could maybe use him when they started building corrals and buying mules and horses.

"Belcher said he's honest, just poor," he told them.

"Well, being poor is not a crime," Chance stated. "And I have no heartburn about helping a man when he's down."

Woody said basically the same thing, but added, "I think it will be a good experience for the boys too. Seeing those Mexican kids in bare feet will do wonders for letting them realize the meaning of being poor. Right now they don't really understand because they've never known poverty."

"You could be right," Curtis answered.

He really had not given any thought to the fact that his boys had never known poverty. For that, he was thankful. He hoped they would never have to live in poverty,—never have to know the hardship and heartache of having to live that kind of life, never have to shed tears because they couldn't provide for their loved ones or have to listen to other people make snide remarks about them and call them "poor white trash." He had known people in his past who had suffered such rudeness and contempt. Even thinking about it now made Curtis upset.

He hoped when they met Juan Diego this Sunday, he would be the sort of man he and his brothers would feel confident having around. For sure they would need help later on and maybe sooner for some of the things they wanted to do on their land. They would know in a few days.

13

Sunday dragged its feet getting there, but it finally arrived. The Demmings met Ron Belcher in front of his Meat Processing Plant just after ten that morning. Curtis introduced his wife and his two boys to Mr. Belcher.

"Nice looking family you have," Belcher commented. "If you folks are ready, I'll lead you to Juan Diego's place. And I am also taking the elk hide."

"Okay, lead on. We'll follow you," Curtis told him.

Curtis fully expected a ton of questions from his boys, but they remained silent as he followed Ron Belcher to the Mexican household. He could see the man standing in the doorway watching them suspiciously as they drove up and parked their vehicles. He couldn't blame the man. The only one he knew was Belcher. The rest were total strangers to him.

Belcher stepped out of his pickup and spoke to the Mexican, "Juan, this is the Demming family I told you about . . . the ones who sent the groceries to you and your family. They want to meet you, so come on over and meet them."

Juan Diego followed Belcher to the vehicles. The men had gotten out of Woody's vehicle and stood beside Curtis now. Curtis extended a hand to shake hands with Juan, as did his brothers.

"I'm pleased to meet you, Mr. Diego," Curtis said. "I wanted to meet you because my brothers and I may have some work for you in the near future, if you're interested. We bought a piece of land west of Walsenburg a short time ago. We are planning to build some sheds and corrals and look into getting some mules or burros and a few horses to break and sell to the miners and anyone else who might want them. Mr. Belcher assured us you are honest. So if you're willing to help us, we will pay you well."

"The name is Juan, amigo. And if I can be of help to you, I'll be proud to work for you. I want to thank you for the food you folks sent out to us. My wife and I really do appreciate it," Juan Diego said.

"We had Mr. Belcher tan the elk hide for you to put on your floor in the house. My wife brought along some cookies for your kids. And she wants to help with clothing and such as you folks might need," Curtis said, turning toward his truck and motioning for Megan and his boys. "Come on out and meet Juan, Megan. You boys can get out of the truck too."

He introduced Megan and his sons to Juan Diego. Megan held out the sack of cookies to him.

"These are for you and your family," Megan told him. "I have a couple of blankets to give you too. And I'd like to meet your wife and kids."

Juan Diego's eyes were brimmed with tears as he took the cookies from Megan. He thanked her and led her to the house where he introduced her to his wife, Lucila. The woman smiled, and Juan spoke to her in rapid Spanish, telling her who this strange woman was and explaining about the menfolk outside and their offer of work for himself. His children sat on the bed, trying to stay covered up against the chill in the one-room house.

Megan could not really tell what sizes they were wearing. She could only guess. But she knew that any that didn't fit she could take back to the Thrift store and get some that did fit. Megan smiled at Lucila. Lucila wouldn't be hard to fit. She asked Juan if it would be all right if she brought them all some clothes and some winter jackets. He looked at her for a long moment.

"We have never had someone be so generous. I cannot afford to pay you for those things, Mrs. Demming. Although I do appreciate the offer," he told her.

"Maybe my husband and his brothers could write it off as an advance payment for the work you will be doing for them," she suggested.

Chance wandered to the door and overheard Megan's suggestion to Juan Diego.

"That's a good idea. Your family needs help to get through the winter, and my brothers and I will be needing help later on. My rifle can keep you in meat along also," Chance stated.

It had been a long, long time since Chance had known a family in such dire need of everything. He had seen a few who were as poor as his Dad and their family had been at one time, but up against this-- their family had been financially blessed!

He and Megan and Juan stepped outside again. Megan took the two blankets from the truck and handed them to Juan.

"This is too much, Mrs. Demming," he protested.

"The name is Megan, and whatever I can do for you and your family, I will do," she told him.

"And so will the rest of us," Woody assured Juan Diego, speaking for the first time.

"Thank you," Juan told them in a near whisper.

Curtis Demming told Juan they had to go but assured him they would be back.

Ron Belcher watched in astonishment. Most people shunned Juan Diego, but here, the whole of the Demming family took them under their wings and treated them like friends and treated them with respect. It was hard for him to fathom, but he was glad he had been able to find help for the Mexican family. He had a feeling it would be a long-lasting relationship.

14

As they drove away, Lorne commented, "That man looked like a scarecrow, Dad."

Curtis chuckled, as did Megan.

"I guess he does, son. He is tall and skinny. But that's only because they are very poor and haven't had enough to eat. And I think it is safe to say both he and his wife have missed some meals so they would be able to feed their kids."

"I wouldn't do that!" Lorne scoffed.

"Yes you would, Lorne, if you had a family and there wasn't enough food to go around to feed you and your kids both. You'd do without to let the kids eat. Let's hope neither you nor Taylor never have to live in poverty and be as poor as that Mexican family is right now," Curtis told his son.

At ten years old, Lorne had never faced such poverty. He didn't know what it was, and he didn't understand the hardships poverty imposed on people. Curtis doubted that Taylor did either. His boys had never known hunger, and he doubted that Juan Diego had known anything but hunger and hard times.

Taylor had been silent the whole trip. Whatever thoughts he had, he kept to himself. But he saw everything. He saw the house that was made mostly of logs with mud chinked into the cracks between them and the holes where the sun had dried the mud and it had chipped away from the logs. He saw insects run in and out of the holes. He saw how dry the ground was around the whole area. He saw how the clothes the Diego family had were worn and hanging on them, partly because they were thin from not eating and partly because that was all they had to wear. A sadness filled his young body. He was glad his family and his uncles didn't have to live like that.

He didn't know that people wouldn't hire Juan Diego because he was Mexican and a very poor Mexican, one who did not have and could not afford good clothes for himself, much less for his family. Taylor did not understand that Juan Diego was too poor to even move his family to a better area.

That evening after supper, Megan began making a list of what she thought she could find at the Thrift shop that might be of use to Juan and Lucila. That included a couple of large pots with lids and a large skillet, clothes, and coats for all of them and maybe some type of quilts or blankets. Maybe even some stuffed toys for the children.

"Megan, what are you doing?" Curtis asked her on his way to the coffeepot.

"Making a list of things I can maybe pick up at the Thrift store for Juan and Lucila and their children," she told him. "I think those kids could do with some stuffed teddy bears too."

He smiled at her. He had not gone inside the house today. He could see some of it through the door from where he stood talking with Ron Belcher. Teddy bears were definitely something he had not seen.

"Let's not forget to get things like tea and cold medicines. The kids will no doubt come down with colds. Some candy canes to eat or for the mother to mix in tea for their ailments. I don't know how bottled water would fare. I didn't see any place they could keep it to keep it from freezing," Curtis said.

"Where do they get water? I didn't see a well or anything," Megan told him.

"Belcher said they get it from a river that runs across the land about a half mile on back from the house. And that's a cold round-trip in the winter," he answered.

Megan felt a shiver run through her body. The fact that anyone would have to walk a half a mile to get water in cold wind and snow in the winter was appalling—and without winter clothes to boot.

Well, they wouldn't be without winter clothes for long if she could help it.

"If they can make it through the winter," Curtis said. "Maybe I can get Woody and Chance to agree to building them a cabin out on our place to live in. There is enough timber on our place to make a nice cabin similar to ours for them to live in. And then we wouldn't have to worry about them not having shelter or clothes or, for that matter, food. We can pay Juan a decent wage, and he can look after what stock we buy to break and sell. He could probably plant a nice garden for them too."

"We'll help them make it through the winter, Curtis," Megan told him, tears glistening in her eyes as she spoke.

* * * * *

The next day after the boys were in school, Megan Demming had her list in her purse and her mind made up as she drove to the Thrift shop. Ann Elkins met her cheerfully as she entered the store.

"Anything I can help you with?" Ann Elkins asked.

"I'm just looking at the minute," Megan replied.

She walked through the store thinking that Ann Elkins could clean the store up some. It wasn't too bad, but it could use cleaning. She paused at the clothing racks and took her time looking through the selections of garments. She found some outfits she thought the Diego children could probably wear. After looking through the Ladies' selections, she found some clothes she thought would fit Lucila. And lastly she found some shirts and a couple of sweatshirts for Juan. She would leave the jeans for Curtis to pick out for him. She was hoping to find coats in their sizes also, but what was hanging in the thrift store were well worn and, in Megan's opinion, should have been trashed. She paid for the items she had picked out and took them to her car.

Next, she drove to a local clothing store where she was able to find socks and underwear for the children. She also found a clearance area where she found coats for the children, along with sweatshirts. She found a nice parka for Lucila and a good lined coat for Juan, for whom she also bought socks and a heavy raincoat for when he had to brave the winter weather to get water for his family.

From the clothing store, she drove to the Five and Dime Variety store. She picked up a set of dishes and tableware, along with some mixing bowls and storage containers for Lucila to put dry food such as oatmeal, sugar, flour, and cereal into, to keep bugs and mice out of them. She completed her list with two large kettles with lids and some saucepans, skillets, spatulas, and wooden spoons. She rounded her shopping out with three plastic tubs in which to put everything in to take to the Diego family.

Curtis came home for lunch and helped her unload her car.

"Did you buy out the whole town?" Curtis asked her teasingly.

"No," she told him. "I only bought half of it!"

But in a serious tone, she told her husband she needed him to buy some jeans for Juan.

"I don't have a clue as to what size to get him or what length the legs need to be."

"I'll take care of it," he told her. "We probably need to take this stuff to them tomorrow. There's supposed to be a storm coming in."

"Okay," she agreed. "Pick up some teddy bears too. I forgot them today."

He laughed and assured her he would come home with jeans and teddy bears.

15

The next day, Curtis loaded the goods going to the Diego family in his truck. There was very little space left in the back seat and back floorboards. He called Chance to see if he would look after Taylor and Lorne after school and told him he and Megan were going back to Pueblo to take the things Megan had bought the day before to the Diego family.

Chance agreed. He got off work an hour before the boys got out of school anyway. He knew Curtis would be late getting back to Walsenburg.

"Hey, how about if me and the boys go ahead and get a tree and bring it home? We could be back by the time you guys are or maybe before," Chance remarked.

"Sounds good. That would assure them of a Christmas tree before that storm hits. Once it gets here, we may not be able to get back to the cabin," Curtis agreed with his brother.

He wished they could cut a small tree for Juan Diego's family, but with everything Megan had bought for them, there probably would not be room for a Christmas tree. Maybe the next year.

Much as he wanted to hurry, he didn't need a speeding ticket so he settled on driving the speed limit. It seemed like the more miles he drove, the farther away Pueblo was. He finally commented on that to his wife. She laughed at him and told him it was just because he was in a hurry to get to the Diego place that Pueblo seemed to be getting farther and farther rather than nearer and nearer.

Once they reached Pueblo, he told Megan, "Let's stop in at the Meat Processing Plant and pick up a few packages of meat to take to them. Lucila can probably use some potatoes and onions and peppers as well as soup seasonings."

"Probably," Megan agreed. "Drop me off at the grocery store, and you can come rescue me after you get them some meat."

He let her out at the grocery store, hoping she didn't go hog wild shopping for things because there wasn't much more room in his truck for any else.

Ron Belcher met him at the Meat Processing Plant. Curtis explained to him what he and Megan were doing and asked for a small box to put a few packaged of meat in to take to them.

"Sure," Belcher said, finding a fairly small box for Curtis to use. "If you don't mind, I'll tag along to their place. I'd like to see their faces when you unload your truck. This is probably the first time in their lives anyone has helped them out or cared about them at all. Besides, maybe I could haul the groceries your missus is buying them."

"Sounds like a plan," Curtis told him. "I wish I had something to cover the outside of their house with. That house looks in desperate need of repair, and I don't think it keeps much of the cold out."

Belcher looked at him and replied, "You know, I think I may have some heavy plastic we could tape up for a temporary cover. Let me look."

He came back in a few minutes with two rolls of tar paper and two rolls of heavy plastic. He disappeared to the back once more and came back with masking tape, hammer and nails, and a ladder. He carried them all out to his own vehicle and loaded it.

Curtis carried his box of meat out to his truck, and Belcher locked the plant.

"Ready when you are," Belcher said cheerfully. "Grocery store, here we come!"

From the looks of the shopping carts Megan had with her, Curtis was glad Belcher had elected to come with them out to the Diego place. They loaded the groceries into Belcher's truck, then followed him to Juan Diego's house.

Juan Diego met them as they descended from their vehicles. His expression was one of surprise at seeing them again so soon.

"To what do I owe this honor, Senors?" he asked them.

Curtis shook hands with him before answering, "Juan, there is a storm coming in, and seeing as to how you folks need so much, we have come to help out. My wife has some clothing and coats for all of you. She also brought some dishes and cookware. And she brought more groceries. We also brought a few packages of meat. Mr. Belcher has some tar paper and heavy plastic we can put around your house to help keep some of the cold out."

Tears came into Juan Diego's eyes.

"But why do you do this for us?" he asked. "Nobody's ever helped us before."

"Then it's time somebody did," Belcher told him. "You can help us cover the sides of your house while Mrs. Demming and your wife get the groceries and things put up and put warmer clothes on the kids."

"Why don't you get into some warmer clothes yourself and put that coat on and you can help us while the women see about the rest?" Curtis said in a tone that was just short of a direct order.

Juan nodded and stepped into his house as Megan came out to get more packages from the truck. Lucila too changed into some warmer clothes and helped her children to dress more warmly.

She set one of the kettles on the stove, put a package of ribs into it, and added water, onions, and potatoes to it. Spotting the packages of carrots, she added a package of those also. She was grateful that their friend from the Meat Processing Plant, who had brought them meat scraps along, had met the Demming family and introduced them to her and Juan.

For many years, she and Juan and their family had survived only because of Mr. Belcher bringing them the meat scraps. Juan had done odd jobs when he could find them and had set snares for small game and, at times, had brought home berries and wild onions. But she and her husband both missed a lot of meals so they could feed their children. At times she had thought they would surely starve to death before nourishment came to them. She smiled at Megan and helped her unpack the groceries and put them on the shelves at one side of the room.

Megan gave a warm smile back, her eyes sparkling. Turning to the children, Megan held up some cookies she baked and gave each of them two to snack on.

It was late by the time the men had the house insulated against the coming storm.

Belcher insisted the last thing to do was wrap the entire house with strips of masking tape placed a foot apart all the way around it.

"It isn't pretty, Juan, but maybe it will help keep you and your family warmer," he said.

As the smell of the cooking meat and vegetables came to them, Curtis asked, "Do you have enough wood, Juan?"

"I will have to gather some more wood," Juan told him.

"Well, how about we take my truck down to the river and gather a load for you?" Curtis suggested.

"Senor, you have done too much already. I can gather the wood," Juan answered.

"Nonsense!" Curtis exclaimed. "Come on, Belcher. With three of us, it won't take long to pick up a load of firewood. Juan, get in."

Along the banks of the Arkansas River, there were plenty of fallen limbs and smaller sticks they could break and use for firewood. They filled the pickup bed and returned to the house. Juan showed them where to unload the truck, and in minutes, they were done.

"I truly appreciate what you have done for me and my family," Juan told Curtis. "Although I do not know why you did it."

Curtis Demming smiled and said softly, "The Lord works in mysterious ways, Juan. You have so little, and while we are not rich, we can help you along. Plus, like I told you earlier, my brothers and I will need your help in a few weeks to build corrals and sheds out on our land."

"I will be there," Juan told him, shaking his hand.

"Meantime, you and your family enjoy a good holiday season. And if you need anything, get a hold of Mr. Belcher and he can get a hold of me or my brothers. We best be getting home, so we'll see you later," Curtis said.

He shook hands with Ron Belcher, thanking him for his help.

Belcher nodded and said, "Between us, we performed a miracle today, and I feel better for having helped out and for knowing Juan and his family have enough to keep them warm and fed."

16

Chance Demming and his two nephews were busy putting decorations on the tree they had decided on and brought home. Chance made a stand for it and set it in a corner of the living room. He helped Taylor and Lorne put strings of lights on it. Now they were excitedly adding bulbs and other types of Christmas decorations to it. He hadn't seen his nephews this excited and happy since they found rocks to start their rock collections. It did his heart good.

They had just finished with the tree when their parents walked through the door. Chance reached down and plugged in the lights and the tree came alive with Christmas beauty.

Curtis and Megan were both surprised. It wasn't hard to see what Chance, Taylor, and Lorne had been busy doing while they were away.

"That's pretty!" Megan exclaimed as she shed her coat.

"Well, we know who to send after the tree next year!" Curtis commented. He had never known Chance to show the kind of excitement he was showing now after finishing helping his nephews find and decorate their Christmas tree. He knew his brother loved the boys, but it was heart-warming to see him smiling and happy at having done this with them.

"Mom, Dad! How do you like the tree?" Taylor asked them, excitement still ringing his voice.

"Us and Uncle Chance found it!" Lorne chimed in, excitement being clear in his voice too.

Both boys were smiling, and so was their Uncle.

"I'd say you guys did a really good job," Curtis told them. "The tree is just the right size, and the decorations are wonderful."

"The boys picked out the decorations for it, including the lights," Chance told him.

"I think they did a good job," Curtis told him. "In fact, all of you did."

"We got some lights to put outside along the roof too. I'll stop by after work tomorrow and help you put them up," Chance said.

"Sounds like you three had a really good day," Curtis remarked. "Chance, maybe you ought to get married and have sons you could enjoy doing things with."

Chance raised an eyebrow and said, "If I could get the kids without the woman, I might take you up on that. I haven't yet seen a woman I'd want to be hitched to, but I do love kids."

"Have you ever thought about checking into the Big Brother program?" Curtis wanted to know.

"No," Chance replied. "I didn't know they had such a thing."

"It might be worth looking into," Curtis told him.

Megan warmed up some soup for supper, and she called them to come eat.

When they sat down at the table, Chance asked Curtis how their day had gone with Juan Diego. Curtis relayed the events of the afternoon.

"Megan did a good job of buying the right sizes of clothes for them, and she also bought dishes and cookware and such for Lucila, and we bought the kids teddy bears, which they loved. Ron Belcher helped me and Juan wrap that house in tar paper and covered that with some heavy plastic wrap Belcher had in his plant. Then we went around it with masking tape, spacing about every ten inches apart to help hold the tar paper and plastic. As I told Juan, it is only temporary insolation. Hopefully, it will help keep them warmer during this storm that's coming in tomorrow. Before we left, we took my truck down to the river where Juan gets his water and picked up a truck load of wood, which we then unloaded near his house."

"It's bound to be warmer than it was the other day," Chance commented.

"I took them several packages of meat, and Megan bought a ton of groceries for them. I told Juan to get a hold of Ron Belcher and have him get a hold of one of us, if he needed us," Curtis added.

"Have you heard anything from Woody today?" he asked Chance.

"No, I haven't. I kept thinking he should be calling anytime now. But maybe he hasn't heard from that Professor yet," Chance replied.

"Could be, I guess," Curtis said. "I'll call him and see if he's heard anything."

"What's up?" Woody answered on the other end of the line.

"I wanted to know if you have heard anything from that Archaeology Professor as yet," Curtis told him.

"No. Not yet," Woody told him. "What have you guys been up to?"

"Taylor and Lorne helped their Uncle Chance find and bring in a Christmas tree that afternoon. They bought lights and decorations too and had it ready to plug in when Megan and I got home," Curtis told him.

"Where were you and Megan?" Woody wanted to know.

"We went to Pueblo. Caught up with Ron Belcher at the Processing Plant. Belcher had some tar paper and heavy plastic and some masking tape and a ladder. We also took some meat and groceries along and went to Juan Diego's place. Megan helped Lucila change the kids into warmer winter clothes. Lucila changed into warmer clothes, and so did Juan. They also dressed the kids in warm clothes. Then Megan helped Lucila put things up and after that Lucila started some meat and vegetable soup. While they were doing that, we men folk put tar paper and plastic around their house and reinforced it with the masking tape at ten-inch intervals around the outside of the house. Then we took my truck down to the river where Juan gets their water from and loaded a truckload of tree limbs for Juan to use in their stove. He showed us where to unload those close to the house. After that, we came home," Curtis informed him. "Why don't you come over and see this Christmas tree?"

"Give me a few minutes," Woody said. "Have you guys eaten?"

"Megan fixed some soup when we got home," Curtis answered.

"I'll stop by the Burger House on my way over," Woody told him and hung up the phone.

If he knew his nephews, they would be starved again by the time he got to their house, and soup had a way of leaving folks hungry again after a few hours. The boys, of course, wouldn't tell their mom they were still hungry. They would just get up after a while and invade the cookie jar, or the chips, or the popcorn and snack until their hunger subsided. He stopped at the Burger House and ordered ten burgers to go with three large orders of french fries. The Burger House, unlike other places, gave an ample serving of french fries. Usually one order was enough for two hungry people. The adults would take what they wanted with their burgers, and the boys would eat like they had tapeworms until the potatoes ran out.

When he entered his brother's house, he asked Megan for a bowl into which to dump the fries and paper plates to divide them onto along with the burgers.

"Woody, you shouldn't have," she told him, although pleased that he had stopped and picked up the burgers and french fries.

She found a bowl to dump the fries into and a pair of aluminum tongs to use in dipping them onto the paper plates beside the burgers Woody was putting on them.

Woody raised his voice and told the others, "Come on and eat these burgers and fries before they get cold."

He didn't have to call them twice.

"Uncle Woody!" Lorne and Taylor both exclaimed as they came into the kitchen, and both threw their arms around him and gave him a hug.

He smiled at them and hugged them back.

"Uncle Woody, have you seen our Christmas tree yet?" Taylor asked him.

"No, not yet, but I will as soon as we eat," he told his nephew. "We'll have to use paper towels. I forgot to get napkins."

"That's fine," Curtis told him.

"Hurry up and eat, Uncle Woody! Uncle Chance helped me and Taylor pick out the tree! Me and Taylor picked out the lights and the ornaments, then Uncle Chance helped us decorate the tree!" Lorne's excitement bubbled over.

"They did a good job of babysitting me this afternoon," Chance told them. "We walked through the woods on Trail Number Four and found this tree. I cut it down and toted it to the pickup, and later the boys found the decorations and I bought them for it. We spent the rest of our time having fun getting it dressed for Christmas."

Curtis winked at Woody, and both smiled and nodded. It had been a long time since either had seen Chance sparkle with happiness. The afternoon had been good for him as well as for the boys.

Taylor and Lorne ate like they hadn't eaten all day and cleaned up the french fries as Woody had known they would. As soon as they had wolfed down the last morsel, they showed Uncle Woody the tree they had helped Uncle Chance with.

Woody looked at it with admiration. His brother and his nephews had done a good job. The tree was beautiful, and he told them so.

17

The next day, Woody received a call at work from Paul Dunhurst, the Archaeology Professor from the Denver University.

"Mr. Demming," he said, "would it be all right for me and my colleague, Charles Krigler, to visit your place on the twenty-eighth?"

"Yes," Woody told him. "I'll let my brothers know. Call me when you get into Walsenburg, and I can let you know where to meet us."

"Okay, Mr. Demming. I'll let you know when we get there. It will probably be around one o'clock when we get there," Mr. Dunhurst told him.

"That's fine, sir. We'll see you then," Woody replied.

Woody then called Chance and Curtis and informed them of Paul Dunhurst's call and relayed his coming to Walsenburg on the twenty-eighth, around noon or shortly thereafter to meet with them, ending with, "I told him to call me when they get here."

Curtis suggested that Woody and Chance meet at his house that Thursday so they would all be together when the Archaeologist arrived and could all ride in one vehicle to meet them somewhere in town and show them the way out to the land and the Indian burial ground they found. Chance and Woody agreed with him.

"I'll call him back and have him call your number," Woody stated.

"Good idea," Curtis told him. "I'll tell Megan. I know she and the boys will want to go, but I think they need to stay home and stay out of the way Thursday."

He told Megan that evening about the Archaeologist coming out that Thursday and that he thought it best if she and the boys stay home that afternoon.

"Day after tomorrow is Christmas Day, so maybe Taylor and Lorne will still be enthralled with their Christmas gifts," he said hopefully.

Megan agreed with her husband. The Archaeology men didn't need the boys getting in their way or asking questions that would detract the men from their work. They didn't need to be going off away from Curtis to search for more rocks for their rock collections. She didn't need either of them getting hurt either.

* * * * *

Christmas fell on a Monday. Megan took a picture of the Christmas tree with its beautiful lights and its many packages wrapped and placed under it. It was a sight to behold. She wanted to be able to remember it for many Christmases to come. That was the first year she had not been involved in helping decorate the Christmas tree.

Taylor and Lorne were up at their usual time. Both bounded down the hallway in their pajamas, and Megan heard excited yelps of joy as soon as they saw the Christmas tree and all the bounty beneath it.

"Can we open our presents now?" Taylor asked her.

"Just one each," she told them. "Your Dad is in the shower, and your uncles are on their way over. As soon as everyone is ready, you can open the rest of your gifts. You might want to also go get dressed."

The boys looked at each other and giggled. Then with excitement flushing their faces, they almost ran back to their rooms to dress.

Curtis came out of his and Megan's bedroom and was almost ran over by his sons on their way back to the Christmas tree. He followed them into the living room.

"Mom told us we can open one gift each until Uncle Chance and Uncle Woody get here," Lorne told his dad.

Curtis grinned and told them to go ahead. Megan had just brought him a cup of coffee when his brothers arrived.

"Looks like we got here just in time!" Chance said.

"Yeah!" Woody agreed. "Any later and we'd have been left out!"

"Have a seat if you can find one," Megan told them as she handed each a cup of coffee.

They all found places to sit and watch the two boys unwrap their gifts. There were new sweaters, new Erector sets, new video games, a skateboard for each, and a new bicycle for each of them. For the men, Megan had bought each a new pair of binoculars and a new winter sweater. Their gifts to her were a set of her favorite perfumes, a new agate necklace with matching earrings, and a new bathrobe.

Having totally forgot about their parents and their uncles, Taylor and Lorne departed for their bedrooms. A few minutes passed as they entered and re-entered each other's rooms. Then with happy smiles on their faces, they emerged.

First they each handed their Mother a stone and a "Merry Christmas," did the same for their Dad, and then to each of their uncles. In return, they each received hugs and a thank you. That made Christmas giving complete. While the adults didn't need the stones they had received from the boys, they were all happy and respected Taylor and Lorne for having given gifts to them.

"I guess I better find something to go with the turkey for dinner," Megan told them.

Woody rose from the chair he had occupied. "I'll fix dinner, Megan. You enjoy your family."

"I'll help," Chance volunteered.

Between them, they furnished a feast that complimented the day.

After they had eaten, Curtis told the boys, "You two find a garbage bag and clean up that wrapping paper from around the Christmas tree."

"Be careful," Taylor cautioned his brother Lorne, "we don't want to step on any of the gifts."

"You hold the bag open," Lorne said. "I'll put the paper in it."

In a few minutes, Lorne stopped and looked at Taylor and asked, "Why don't we put our things in our room?"

Taylor agreed, and they very carefully took their new bicycles and skateboards to their rooms first then gathered the rest of their gifts and deposited them on top of their beds. It was much easier to finish picking up the wrapping papers that remained on the floor.

* * * * *

The next morning, Curtis called the Sheriff and filled him in about the burial ground and what Professor Dunhurst told Woody. He asked him if he and the Coroner could meet with them Thursday, just after noon around one, to meet the Professor and the State Archaeologist and go with them to the site on the Demming property where they found the burial ground.

"Be glad to, and I'll drag the Coroner along," the Sheriff told him.

18

Thursday morning, Chance and Curtis both joined Woody at his house. They sat drinking coffee, nibbling on some store-bought cookies and speculating about what time they thought the Professor might call.

It was nearly ten o'clock when the Archaeology Professor, Paul Dunhurst, called Woody. He had his friend, Charles Krigler, with him, he told Woody. They just pulled into the Sinclair gas station in Walsenburg.

"Stay right there, and we will be there in about ten minutes," Woody told him.

As he hung up the phone, he told his brothers, "That was Mr. Dunhurst. He and his friend are waiting for us at the Sinclair station on Main Street."

"Okay," Chance said. "Let's go see what we got."

Curtis followed him to his vehicle, and Woody climbed into the back seat.

Chance turned the engine on when Woody said, "Wait a minute. I forgot the camera. We might as well take it. I'll be right back."

It didn't take Woody long to come back with his camera and get into the back seat again. A few minutes later, Chance pulled into the Sinclair station. They saw the vehicle with the Denver County tags and parked beside it. There was no one in it, and the Demming brothers assumed the Archaeologists were inside. They waited, knowing the men would return before long. The Sheriff pulled in beside them, and he had the Coroner with him.

When they came out of the building, Paul Dunhurst introduced Charles Krigler to the three Demming brothers. They in turn introduced Sheriff Nelson and the Coroner, Lance Holland.

They all shook hands, then Curtis told them, "If you guys will follow us, we'll take you to the Indian graves we found on the property we bought a few months ago."

"Lead on!" Dunhurst said excitedly, and they all loaded.

Paul Dunhurst followed Chance out to their land.

* * * * *

Chance stopped at the cabin. He got out of his vehicle and walked over to Dunhurst.

"I haven't been through here with my pickup," he told the Professor. "I don't know how rough it will be to get across to the burial ground."

"That's fine. I'll just take it easy and follow you out to it," Dunhurst told him.

Chance drove slowly, not wanting to damage either vehicle en route to the burial ground. Once, he had his brothers get out and move large rocks out of the way so they could pass more easily. He came to the old road and turned toward the ancient graves.

He stopped a few feet back from them. Once they were out of his vehicle, Woody took a photo of them. That gave them a before photo from which they could have copies made if necessary.

Paul Dunhurst and Charles Krigler both stepped out of their vehicle and walked a few feet forward.

"How did you gentlemen find these old burial graves?" Dunhurst ask them.

"We were walking through the land we had bought, along with my sons and my wife, when we came upon them," Curtis told him. "We didn't know they were here until then. There was no mention of them when we bought the land."

"Let me get some pictures of them, and then we'll get some close-up pictures also," Charles Krigler said.

He knelt to get straight, forward photos of the ones on the edge. Then he took pictures of the side of the burial ground. He also took a close-up photo of a single grave.

Sheriff Nelson also took some photos.

"Do you know what tribe of Indians these might be from?" Curtis wanted to know.

Krigler looked at him and said, "No. There were many tribes who migrated back and forth over this land in the past. I suspect they may be Cherokee. We will have to get a State License to Excavate one of them to have their bones analyzed, as will whatever items may have been buried with them."

"Could this have been a small village of some tribe or maybe some who had become ill and left behind?" Curtis asked.

Sheriff Nelson told them he didn't believe these were Indian graves. "The Indian tribes here in Colorado don't mark their graves that I know of."

"Why is that?" Dunhurst asked him.

"Because there is too much thievery that goes on. People rob the graves of sacred items, and have been known to dig up the skeletal remains of the person buried there."

"I think the best thing we can do is have one of them excavated and see what comes out of having the bones and personal things analyzed," Paul Dunhurst spoke to them. "It will take time to get a License to Excavate the grave. But that is the only sure way we will know the exact data we need. These graves are very old and may have well been among those with disease. I counted thirty-two graves, and some were children from the looks of things."

"That's what I counted too," Charles Krigler confirmed. "Let's measure the graves, and then we'll measure the area around them. After that, I will put small stakes at the corners with yellow strips in them. That way they will be easier to find next time."

"We can fence the burial site if you want us to," Curtis offered.

"Let's wait and see if we can get permission to excavate one grave first. There's no sense in building a fence that would have to be torn down later," Krigler told him. "I will need the legal of your land to put in my report."

Curtis Demming gave the property legals to the archaeologist.

To this point, the Coroner had not said anything. Now he informed all of them that the Indians did not make burial mounds anywhere in Colorado, so he believed these were historical graves of some sort. If that proved to be true, there may not be anything more the Archaeologist could do.

"That could be true," Krigler commented. "We will check with the National Register of Historical Places and see what we can come up with. I still need to make a report of this site even if we are unable to advance further with our information."

Krigler went to the vehicle he and Paul Dunhurst were using and took out a folder of papers. He took out one sheet, laid it on top of the folder, put the entire folder on the hood of the pickup, and began filling it in.

"I may have to have all your signatures later on," he told them. "Right now, I want to fill in the necessary forms and get them sent in to the State Archaeology Department and see if we can obtain a License to Evacuate."

"As I said, it may take some time," Krigler said. "I will keep in touch with you, gentlemen. I think I have all I need for now. Thank you for contacting us and for showing this site to us. You have a nice place."

"Thanks. We call this part of it 'Trail Number Four.' It just makes it easier to know what area we are talking about when we talk of it," Curtis told him.

The eagle flew overhead, screaming at them to leave his territory. They had no business invading and bringing more humans with them. He didn't want them here.

Krigler and Dunhurst both shook hands with the Demming brothers and with the Sheriff and the Coroner before leaving.

Curtis looked at his brothers. "Sounds like it may be a while before we know anything about this site. This being the holiday season for a few more days, I doubt if any of the State offices will be open."

"I have an idea you're right," Woody told him.

"I think these are some type of prehistoric mounds," Sheriff Nelson told them. "I don't believe that Archaeologist will be able to obtain a license or even some kind of permit that will allow evacuation of any of them."

"How many Indian tribes live in or lay claims to Colorado?" Chance asked him.

"The last I knew, there were about twenty-five. And if I'm wrong about those mounds, that Archaeologist has his work cut out for him. He will have to have permission to excavate from the head Chiefs of every one of those tribes," the sheriff informed him.

"Well, thanks for coming out. And thank you, too, Mr. Holland, for coming out," Curtis told them and shook hands with both of them before they got into the Sheriff's car to leave.

"Let's stop back by the cabin and check it out before we go home," Chance suggested. "That way, we can check and make sure nothing has been disturbed and also use the outhouse while we're there."

"Good idea," Curtis commented.

* * * * *

When they arrived back at Curtis Demming's house, his wife and his boys were anxious to know what the Archaeologists had told them about the Indian burial site.

Her husband and his brothers filled her in as much as they could, and Curtis ended the explanations with, "It may be a while before Mr. Krigler will know whether or not he can obtain the License to Excavate one of the graves to have scientific studies and lab analogies done. They can't excavate without a license."

"I see," Megan answered.

"Will we be able to watch when they dig up the grave?" Taylor asked his dad.

"No, son. And I don't know that they'll want us men folk out there either," Curtis told him.

"But we could stay in the truck, and we wouldn't be in the way," Lorne put in.

"Lorne, I know you both mean well, but the answer is still no," Curtis answered his youngest son.

He saw the disappointment in their faces, but they would just have to live with that for now.

19

"Are you two off tomorrow?" Curtis asked his brothers.

"I have to work to make up for taking a personal day today so I could go with you and Chance," Woody told him.

"I get off at eleven tomorrow. What did you have in mind?" Chance replied.

"You want to go with me to Pueblo to check on Juan and his family and pick up some meat to bring home?" Curtis asked him.

"Sure. We better take some vegetables and fruits to them also," Chance said.

"I can do that and be ready to leave when you get here," Curtis commented.

"Sounds like a plan. I'll be here when I get off work," Chance told his brother.

"I'll see if Megan will bake their kids some cookies," Curtis told him.

"Well, I'll see you guys tomorrow evening then," Woody said as he headed for the door.

Megan overheard Curtis tell Chance he'd see if she would bake some cookies for Juan's kids. She smiled at him and told him she would have Taylor help her. That would give him a start on his decision to learn how to cook.

"Bake lots because you know Lorne has a hollow toe," Chance told her with a smile.

She laughed at him and said, "That's not all—he has some Uncles that have hollow toes too!"

Chance laughed as he went to the door to leave. He didn't know how Curtis got so lucky as to find a rose among the thorns.

* * * * *

The next morning, Megan had Taylor help her in the kitchen. She got out the recipe for homemade sugar cookies and laid it on the cabinet. Then she told her son what ingredients to get out that he was going to need.

"How come you have to get all the stuff out, Mom?" he asked.

"So you don't have to hunt for it as you go," she explained as she got out two big mixing bowls.

"What are those for?" Taylor asked.

"One is for mixing the dry ingredients into. That's the flour, sugar, baking powder, salt, and cinnamon. Measure each one according to the recipe. In the other bowl, mix the eggs, the oil, and the vanilla. Turn the oven on to 375 degrees so it can be getting warm while you slowly mix the dry mixture into the liquid. Your batter should be fairly thick. At least thick enough that you can use a spoon to place the cookie dough onto the cookie sheet.

"You can use a table knife to push the dough off the spoon where you want it on the cookie sheet. Space them at least two inches apart. And when the cookie sheet is full, put it in the oven and set the timer for about twelve minutes. While the cookies are baking, get a bath towel and a spatula. Spread the towel out on the table, and when the cookies come out of the oven use the spatula to put them onto the towel to cool," Megan told her son.

"Can you help me with them, Mom?" Taylor asked.

"No, Taylor. I'm going to sit back and watch and let you make them. Remember, you wanted to learn to cook. And cookies are the easiest things to start with," his mother told him.

She refilled her coffee cup and sat down at one end of the table where she could watch Taylor mix his first batch of sugar cookies.

The first batch of cookies came out of the oven, and Lorne came out of his room.

"Mmm! Those smell good! Can I have one?" he asked.

"No, Lorne. These are going to Juan and his family," his mother told him. "We'll make some more later for us, and then you can have one."

"Oh. Okay. Where's Dad?" Lorne wanted to know.

"He's gone to the store to pick up some fruits and vegetables for Lucila. He'll be back pretty soon. Then when Uncle Chance gets off work, he and your dad are going to Pueblo and check on Juan and his family, and they will also bring us home some meat," she explained to her youngest son.

"When Taylor gets through with the cookies, can we play with our skateboards?" Lorne wanted to know.

"If Taylor feels like it," Megan told him.

Taylor looked at Lorne with a smile. They hadn't played with the skateboards since opening them at Christmas. Today there was no ice or snow on the sidewalks. It should be a good day to have fun with them. His younger brother could sometimes come up with some good ideas.

Both boys were outside riding their skateboards when Curtis got home from the grocery store. They were about a half a block away and having a good time when Curtis drove up. They saw him and came back to the house.

"Hey, Dad! Guess what? Taylor made the cookies!" Lorne told him excitedly. "Mom's gonna let him make some more after you and Uncle Chance go to Pueblo!"

"Well, I'm sure they'll be good if Taylor made them," Curtis commented.

"Mom wouldn't let us eat any. She said we could have some of the next ones," Lorne went on.

"That's because these are for Juan's family," Taylor told him.

"Sounds like you'll have plenty to eat later," Curtis told them.

Chance was not long in getting there, and he got the same reception from the nephews that his brother had gotten.

He smiled at them and said, "Be sure you leave your Dad and me some of the cookies you bake this afternoon. We'll be hungry when we get back."

"Sure thing, Uncle Chance!" Taylor responded.

Curtis had heard his brother drive up, and as Chance parked behind his vehicle, he took the groceries out of his pickup and put them on the back seat and floor board of his brother's pickup.

As he got in with Chance, he told his sons, "You guys be good. And take care of your Mother."

"We will, Dad!" they said almost in unison.

The day was pleasant but cool. The sky overhead was clear and blue, with the exception of a couple of small clouds. The traffic toward Pueblo was light, and they made good time.

20

They met very few vehicles on their way to Pueblo, which was unusual for a Friday. Chance stopped at the Meat Processing Plant. They got out and went inside where Ron Belcher met them.

"How have you gentlemen been?" he asked jovially.

Curtis handed the locker key to Chance, and while his brother picked out several pieces of meat for Juan, he told Belcher about the Archaeologist visiting their place west of Walsenburg.

"You mean there is an actual old Indian burial ground on your place?" Belcher was surprised to hear about it.

"Yes, we think that's what it is, and as far as we know, it has never before been reported to anyone," Curtis told him.

"So what are the Archaeologists going to do about it?" Belcher asked.

"Krigler is the Archaeologist. Dunhurst is an Archaeology Professor at the University in Denver," Curtis corrected him. "Krigler is going to contact the State and see about getting a license or at least a permit to excavate one of the graves so they can run DNA samples both on the body and the articles buried with it. If he does get a permit to evacuate one of the graves, he may have to send or take the articles out of state to a lab somewhere to have the DNA testing done. I don't think I've ever heard of DNA testing having been done in Colorado."

Chance came back out of the locker room with a box of packaged meats. He gave the key back to his brother.

"We're going out to Juan's place. You want to ride out with us?" Curtis asked the proprietor of the Meat Processing Plant.

Ron Belcher looked surprised but agreed to go. He himself had not had a chance to go out there since he and Curtis had wrapped the house in tar paper and thick plastic to help insulate it against the winter weather.

* * * * *

Juan Diego came outside when he heard them drive up. He shook hands with all three of them.

"Juan, how've you been? And how's your family?" Curtis Demming asked him.

Juan smiled and told him Mateo had a bad cold, but so far the rest were okay.

"Well, give us a hand here, and we'll get these groceries unloaded. Megan sent some cookies for the kids," Curtis said.

"You are too good to us, Senor," Juan Diego commented, picking up a sack of groceries and helping carry them into his house.

"Has this temporary wrapping helped keep your house warmer?" Belcher asked him.

"Si, Senor! It has helped much!" Juan replied.

Luis and Manuela wore smiles and bright eyes. Mateo smiled, but his eyes were filled with fever from his cold. That didn't stop him from eating two of the cookies Megan had sent along.

"Juan, let's go gather another truckload of wood and let Lucila put up her groceries," Curtis suggested.

It took the men almost an hour to fill Chance's pickup bed with usable firewood, and Juan helped them unload it in the same area they had unloaded the last load.

"Next time, I'll bring my chain saw and trim up some of the trees along that creek. Then I can cut those limbs up into firewood for you, Juan," Chance stated.

They heard Mateo coughing when they finished emptying out the bed of Chance's truck.

"Do you have some cold medicine for Mateo's cold?" Curtis asked Juan.

"Lucila made some cough medicine from a Mexican recipe her mother used," Juan answered.

"Something you might try—something Mom used to give us boys years ago—is to slice and onion, put a little bit of sugar between the slices, and let it set over night. The sugar draws the juice from the onion. Mom used to give us boys one teaspoon at a time whenever she thought we needed it, which was probably about every four hours, even though it seemed like it was every few minutes. You might try that for Mateo," Curtis suggested.

Juan nodded, saying, "Gracias, Senor. We will try that. And thank you for helping me and my family. We are truly humbled by your help. No one else has ever done anything for us."

"You are welcome, Juan. We have to be getting back now, but we'll see you again soon," Curtis replied.

On the way back to Pueblo, Ron Belcher commented, "Well, Juan's family looks a little better than they did last time, even the little boy with the cold. I'm glad we wrapped that house for them. I can't imagine living there, and especially not the way it was. Those folk were literally freezing and starving to death before you guys came along."

Chance and Curtis looked at Belcher and smiled.

"If you hadn't told us about them and showed us where they live, they would have starved to death," Curtis said. "In that respect, you helped as much as we have."

They stopped back by the Meat Processing Plant, and Curtis went back to the locker room and picked out several packages of meat to take home to his and Megan's freezers.

When he came back to the front of the store, he shook hands with Belcher, telling him, "We'll see you next time."

Megan had a beef and vegetable stew on the warm setting on the stove when Curtis and Chance came in. Tantalizing odors from the pot filled the house, and both just remembered they had not eaten all day.

"That stew sure smells good, Megan. Are we too late to get a some of it?" her husband asked her.

She smiled and told him, "Not quite, but I was thinking of throwing it out back for the birds!"

"Don't you dare!" Chance exclaimed. "I'd have to turn into a bird if you did that, and I have enough trouble trying to act like a human!"

Still smiling, she sat large bowls of stew on the table for them, then brought them crackers and fresh lemonade to go with it.

"How were Juan's family?" she asked them.

"Looking better. But little Mateo has a cold and a bit of fever," Curtis told her.

"We took them some meat, which, by the way, I brought home some for us. It's still in the truck. We also picked up another load of fire wood and brought it to the house for Juan."

"I'm glad they're doing better. The first time I saw them, it almost made me cry," she told him. "I'll have Taylor bring the meat in. You two finish eating."

21

L ater that week, Professor Paul Dunhurst called Woody Demming.

"Mr. Krigler called to say the State license is pending the reply from the Physical Anthropologist," the Professor told him. "He is the person who conducts the Forensic Osteology, and he is also the person who will need to be on hand do the excavation because he will then, when the skeletal remains are taken to the laboratory, execute the remains a human skeletal analysis. But—and this is a big *but*—the State of Colorado does not have a Forensic lab, and DNA is not allowed here. The nearest lab is at the University of Arizona."

"I see," Woody commented. "And if they are Indian burial graves?"

"He will also have to try to find the tribes that lived in that area and get at least one member of each tribe to join us at the burial site when they do the excavation," Dunhurst went on. "And that, Mr. Demming, could take considerable time. You see, tribes have their own rules about Sacred Sites. That's what they call their burial grounds. And some are not allowed to talk about them even. Many of them believe their ancestors' spirits are still present at these places. There are some twenty-five tribes that claim that area of Colorado their ancestral lands."

"My brothers and I didn't think about that," Woody told the Professor truthfully.

"Don't be discouraged. You gentlemen did the right thing in reporting the burial site. It just might take a lot longer than any of us anticipated. I will let you know as soon as I know something more to tell you," Dunhurst assured him.

"Thank you, Mr. Dunhurst. We'll be looking forward to hearing from you when you find out something. I want you to know we really appreciate all your help with this," Woody told him.

"You're more than welcome," Dunhurst said and hung up the phone.

Woody Demming called his younger brother and asked him if he and Curtis could meet at Curtis's house that evening.

"I'll call Megan so she will be expecting all of us. Why do you want us to meet this evening?" Curtis asked.

"I just got off the phone with Professor Dunhurst. I thought you and Chance would want to hear about it," Woody told him.

"I'll call Chance. He's probably home by now," Curtis replied.

"Okay. See you then," Woody told him.

Curtis called Chance first and let him know to be at his house for supper because Woody had some information to share with them from Professor Dunhurst.

Curtis then called his wife and told her, "Whatever you are fixing for supper, make it in triplicate. You have two starving brothers-in-law coming over. Woody has some information to share with us."

"Okay, honey. I have a squash casserole about ready for the oven. I can do some chicken fried steaks and mashed potatoes with white gravy and maybe some creamed peas. I baked a fresh apple pie this morning. So I think we'll have enough," Megan replied.

"You keep talking, and I'll be taking off early to come home," Curtis teased her.

Megan didn't make a habit of making fresh fruit pies for dessert. Usually they were bought at the bakery in town. The bakery made really good pies, and he had no complaints about their pies. But Megan had them beat six ways to Sunday when she was in a mood to bake.

Chance arrived before Woody did and asked what their meeting was all about. He followed Curtis into the living room, and Megan gave them both a cup of coffee. Curtis let him know Woody had heard from Dunhurst and wanted to tell them about it. Taylor and Lorne burst into the living room and, after giving hugs to their Uncle Chance, asked him why he came over.

"Your Uncle Woody has some things to tell us," Chance informed his nephews. "He'll be here in a few minutes."

"We will probably discuss whatever Woody needs to tell us over supper. So you boys will need to be quiet," Curtis told his sons.

Both boys assured him they would be quiet. They wanted to hear what their Uncle Woody had to say too. They felt a bit of importance at being allowed to listen with the adults to what Uncle Woody had to say, especially if it was about that Indian burial ground they had found that the boys weren't allowed to search for treasures for their rock collections.

Woody wasn't long in getting there. He had taken time to grab a shower and a clean set of clothes before coming over to his brother's house.

As they filled their plates and gathered around the table, Woody told them about the call from Professor Dunhurst.

"He said it may take longer than any of us anticipated to get the State to issue a permit so they can evacuate a grave. The Archaeologist—that is, Mr. Krigler—has to contact what they call a Physical Anthropologist. That person will have to be there before they can exhume the graves," Woody explained. "And if I understood him correctly, the nearest one of those persons is in Arizona."

"What's an Anthropologist?" Taylor asked in spite of telling his Dad he and his brother would be quiet.

"That's a person who will excavate the skeletal remains and get the DNA readings so we can find out what tribe these Indians were a part of," Woody said.

"But," Woody went on to explain, "this may take some time. If, as we believe, these are ancient Indian graves, there has to be a member of each tribe who lived in that area present at the burial site. That could take a while because, as the Sheriff pointed out, there were about twenty different tribes that claim Ancestral Rights to that land. And you see, each tribe has different religious and sacred beliefs. Plus, it would have to be the Chief of each tribe having to be present to give permission to excavate a grave. Depending on their beliefs, they may not allow the grave to be dug up."

"Why wouldn't they let the grave be excavated?" Curtis asked. "It looks like they would want to know, just like we do, who the burial site belongs to."

Woody nodded. He went on to explain that some Indian tribes believe the spirits of their ancestors are still present at these burial sites to protect them from being disturbed.

"And while the Ute Indians were the primary tribe that lived in southern Colorado, there were other tribes that lived in this region off and on while hunting, such as the Navajo and the Mohave and some others also," Woody told them. "It is mandatory by law that a member of each tribe has to be present and they all have to agree to the excavation before it can be done."

"Wow! That could take months or even years," Chance stated.

"Dunhurst told me he will call again when he has something more to report," Woody commented. "We will just have to wait and see what turns up."

"There doesn't seem to be anything else we can do for now," Chance replied.

"I'm glad the Professor called to let us know where things stand at this time," Curtis Demming agreed.

"I have a question," Lorne said.

"What is it you want to know?" his Dad asked him.

"I want to know if the Indians wore fig leaves like Adam and Eve did in the Bible?" Lorne told him.

That drew laughter from everyone except Lorne. But when the laughter stopped, his Uncle Woody told him no.

"The Indians used animal furs to make clothing. They sometimes traded buffalo and other hides to the Trading Posts for blankets and food items. They wove baskets to use when they went hunting for berries or herbs or medicinal barks and roots. Some of their baskets were also used for water storage and to store food in. They made shoes and ropes and I'm sure other things also from the yucca plant," he explained to his nephew.

"What's a yucca plant?" Lorne asked.

"I'll show you one the next time we go to the cabin," Uncle Woody told him.

Now it was Taylor's turn to ask a question.

"What did the Indians use for food besides meat when there were no trading posts around?"

Woody had to smile. "They used several different types of lily roots, they knew where wild onion grew, they used a plant known to us as the Indian potato, one they called the Indian carrot, they knew what seeds were eatable, they gathered various types of berries, they gathered whatever kinds of nuts they could find, they knew what flowers were eatable, and they used the fruits of the prickly pear cactus."

The boys looked at each other then again at their Uncle Woody.

"Boy, Uncle Woody, you sure are smart!" Taylor remarked.

"You boys might see if your school library has information about the Indians," he suggested to them. "If it doesn't, then we'll find time to visit the public library one of these days. You can learn a lot by reading books about the Indians."

"Can we do that, Dad?" Lorne asked with excitement rising in his voice.

"I'll bet we can," he told them. "Now you boys quit pestering your Uncle Woody."

Chance hadn't said anything until now, but addressing his nephews, he said to them, "You boys can find a lot of information on your computers. Put what you want to know in the address bar, and it will usually come up with some type of information or refer you to another website that will give you some answers."

Both boys smiled at him and told him, "Thanks, Uncle Chance!"

Uncle Chance had just given them a whole new world to explore.

22

Valentine's Day came in blustery and cold and a few degrees below zero. In spite of that, Megan Demming had baked sugar cookies for the boys to take to school for their classmates. And she had put back two dozen to be taken to the Diego family the next time the men decided to take groceries to them.

The evening left them with falling snow that promised to stay around for a few days more. And true to its promise it lingered for three days dumping ten inches of snow for them to deal with.

Curtis Demming called Ron Belcher to ask about the weather in Pueblo.

"We've had light snow the past few days, but it was mostly south of us," Belcher told him. "We have to watch out for black ice in spots, but most of the roads are passable."

"Would you mind too much taking some meat to Juan Diego and his family? And if you could pick up some soup and cans of vegetables for them also, I will pay you when I can get through to come to Pueblo," Curtis said, explaining they were pretty much snowed in there in Walsenburg for a couple more days at least.

"I don't mind doing that at all," Belcher told him. "In fact, if I start right now I should be able to get back before the roads get icy again."

"Thanks," Curtis Demming told him, wondering if Juan still had enough firewood.

He and Chance had cut a lot the last trip over there, but with the cold and now the subzero temperatures nature had thrown at them, it would take a lot of wood to keep even a small house warm.

He was relieved that Ron Belcher agreed to take food to them. They probably were running low on groceries as well.

The phone rang, bringing Curtis back to today. He answered it to find his brother Woody on the phone.

"What's up?" Curtis asked.

"Curtis, can you come over and help me get my pickup started?" Woody asked him.

"Sure, Woody. Let me get my jumper cables, and I'll be right there," Curtis told his brother.

He started his own pickup and let it idle while he got his jumper cables from the garage. Minutes later, he was on his way to help Woody get his vehicle started. It was a good thing Woody had a large front yard because Curtis had to turn his vehicle so that his cables would reach both pickup batteries. He lifted the hood of his pickup and connected the cables to the battery in his vehicle, then Woody connected the other ends of the cables to the battery in his pickup. While they waited for the battery in Woody's vehicle to charge, Curtis had Woody get inside his vehicle out of the cold and told him about calling Ron Belcher to have him take food out to Juan Diego's family.

"That's good, Curtis. There's no way we can get through to Juan right now. I suspect they are low on groceries by now," Woody replied. "I was going to try to go to work, but my pickup didn't agree with me. Thanks for coming over. Let's see if she'll start now."

His pickup started, and he decided to let it run for a few more minutes. He thanked Curtis again and went inside the house.

*　*　*　*　*

Curtis Demming drove to the school his boys were attending. Chances were that school either would cancel or let out early. There were only a few students already there when he had taken Taylor and Lorne to school earlier. As he pulled up by the school, the boys came running out to the truck and hurriedly got into the vehicle.

"I'm sure glad you came back, Dad! They canceled school today! The principal was going to try to drive everyone home in a few more minutes," Taylor told him. "I called Mom, and she said you went to help Uncle Woody. So I called Uncle Woody, and he said you had left his place. So you must have had your ESP working!"

Curtis smiled at his son knowingly. How does one explain to a kid how you just sometimes play a hunch?

"I just had a feeling that you might not have school today," he said.

Once home from school, both Taylor and Lorne went immediately to their rooms and turned on their computers. They tried to find out what kind of rocks they had picked up out at the cabin. As they found a few of them, they also found out about the area around Walsenburg. Both were intrigued with learning about the Wet Mountain area, which was also referred to as the Greenhorn Mountains in the northwestern area of Huerfano Park, and of the mountain range known as the Spanish Peaks southwest of Walsenburg and of the San de Cristo Mountains to the west of Walsenburg along the eastern slopes of the Rocky Mountains. Among the rocks both of them had gathered so far were pieces of perlite, quartz, sandstone, lava, schist, and small pieces of shale. Their excitement echoed throughout the house.

Taylor, followed by his younger brother, went to the study where his father was working on some ledgers and asked, "Dad, one of these days when you have time, can we go explore the Huerfano Park?"

Curtis looked up from his work and, seeing the hopeful and excited faces of his sons, told them calmly, "Maybe this summer when you boys are out of school."

Both came to him and showered him with hugs and thank-you's. He hadn't seen them that excited since they had first began gathering rocks out on the land surrounding the cabin. He was glad to see that they were taking an interest in learning about the area near where they lived. It was gratifying to know they were learning on their own without having to be told, even if it was their Uncle Chance who planted the seed of this new world for them.

Early afternoon brought a call from Woody again. This time, it was to inform Curtis that the Archaeology Professor Paul Dunhurst had called. The State Archaeologist, Charles Krigler, had called Mr. Dunhurst to let him know he was still working at finding ancestors of the people buried at the old burial site on their land. He had stated that it may be impossible to find any of their ancestors as the burial mounds in the United States were larger, wider, longer, and taller mounds, and mostly in the eastern United States. That the mounds the Demming brothers found were so much smaller indicated an era some 1,200 years ago, predating the larger mounds in his research. The only other solution Mr. Krigler could come up with was that that may have been a small village wiped out by a warring faction and buried with what rock was available at the time to keep predators out and was never recorded anywhere at the time it had happened.

In which case, the State may have to mark the area as an Unknown Historical Burial Site and leave it at that. They may not put up any kind of a marker, just leave it as it is, and let the Demming brothers take care of it. But he also said that Krigler is looking into the possibility that those graves could conceivably be Cherokee Indian graves. It seems there were some Cherokee Indians living in Colorado during the 1800s and they did cover their ancestors graves with stones to keep predators from digging up the graves and also to keep their spirits from haunting the living.

"Krigler is still researching it, and Dunhurst told me he will call again when Mr. Krigler finds out more about it and has information he can share," Woody concluded.

"If the State just has to mark it as an Unknown Historical Site or doesn't see the need to mark it, then we'll fence it so my boys and others won't disturb the graves," Curtis told him.

"Okay," Woody agreed. "Let me call Chance. I'm sure he'll agree with us on that."

"Tell Chance he opened a whole new world for his nephews. They spent all morning on their computers looking for the kinds of rocks they had gathered and learned a lot about the Huerfano Park area. They are excited and want to go see it later on. I told them maybe when school is out. They did this on their own without Megan or me having to tell them to do it. So I'm proud of them for that," Curtis told his brother.

"I always knew Chance was good for something! Tell the boys I'm proud of them too. I know Chance will be. Talk to you later," Woody responded.

23

It was mid-March already and time for Curtis to get his files ready for the tax preparer. It wasn't his favorite time of the year. He tried to keep his ledgers and files straight, but it seemed he invariably missed something somewhere in them. But at last, he thought he finally had them ready to take to the accountant.

He left his study and went into the living room and sat down in a chair next to his wife. She was watching a John Wayne movie with their sons. He settled back in the chair and relaxed and finished watching the last half of it with them.

He wanted to go check on Juan Diego and his family. Most of the snow from the past few weeks was gone, and even though a light snow was falling now, he believed he could get through to Pueblo and Juan Diego's place. When the movie was over, he mentioned his thoughts to Megan.

"That's a good idea, Curtis," she said. "Maybe Chance can go with you this time and help out with groceries and firewood for them. Hopefully little Mateo is over his cold by now."

Curtis called Ron Belcher to see if he could put together a box of frozen meat for tomorrow. Belcher told him it would be ready by the time he got there and that he could go along if Curtis wanted him to.

He turned from the phone and asked Megan if she wanted to go grocery shopping with him.

"Sure," she told him.

"You boys want to go shopping with us? Or would you want to stay home and finish watching TV?" Curtis asked Taylor and Lorne.

They both opted to stay home. They had been waiting all week to see the movie that was just coming on now. Besides, it was cold outside, and who wants to spend the afternoon getting in and out of the cold, especially when there was a good movie to watch?

At the grocery store, both Megan and Curtis took a shopping cart through the store.

Curtis asked the store manager if they could buy canned goods by the case.

"That's highly unusual," the store manager stated, asking them why they wanted to buy canned goods by the case.

Curtis explained to him they were helping a poor family, and with the winter weather being what it was, he wanted to be sure they had groceries for a while, in case they couldn't get through to deliver the food to them.

"Tell me what canned goods you want, and I'll see what we have in the back," the store manager told him.

Curtis handed the man the list he had made that included beef and vegetable soup and canned fruits.

"Give me a few minutes, and I'll see what we have. I'll bring out a case of what we have of each item you have on the list," the store manager told him.

Curtis thanked him and told him they would wait right where they were until he returned.

It was ten minutes before the store manager came back escorting a hand truck with several cases of vegetables, a case of beef vegetable soup, a case of sliced peaches and sliced pineapple, and a case of orange juice.

"This is all the extra cases I could scrape up in the back," he said.

"That's great. We'll take all of it, plus the rest of what we have in our carts," Curtis told him.

"I'll roll this to the register for you," offered the store manager.

Again, Curtis thanked him.

At the register, the store manager told the cashier to go take a break and he himself rang out the groceries, reducing the cases of canned goods to half price, for which Curtis Demming was glad. But he still had almost three hundred dollars' worth of items.

"I really appreciate this, sir," he told the store manager.

"You are very welcome," the man replied, helping Curtis take the groceries outside to his truck.

They put the cased goods in the bed of the truck and the rest on the back seat. Curtis knew he would have to unload the truck tonight and reload it in the morning, but that was okay. The Diego family would have food for the coming weeks. And if they got another deep snow, which was likely, he wouldn't have to worry about them having enough to eat.

As an after-thought, he stopped by the Mercantile store and bought two one-hundred-foot tarps and some ties to fasten them together with. This was only mid-March, and he wasn't sure the heavy tar paper and heavy plastic they had insulated the Diego house with was enough to keep it warm in the months to come. They had been lucky so far that they only had cold in the low thirties and only a couple of snowstorms, but the end of March and the month of April could change the weather into real winter, with the howling, cold wind and freezing temperatures. They should have already thought of the tarps, but it still would not be too late to put them over the other. If he could get Chance to follow him in his truck, they could also pick up some insulation to put between the plastic and the tarps and maybe a couple of area rugs to put on the floor over the elk skin to help keep their feet warmer.

He expressed his thoughts to his wife on their way home. She listened as he talked, and when he asked her what she thought of it, she smiled and said, "I think you are an angel and that God sent you to look after that family!"

He smiled back at her. He could have searched for a long time and never found another woman like Megan.

His eyes sparkled, and he told her gently and sincerely, "I love you, Megan. You're the angel God sent to me."

"What were you thinking of getting Taylor for his birthday?" Megan asked.

"I don't know. I really hadn't thought about it," Curtis answered.

"You better think about it. His birthday is in two days," Megan reminded him. "He will be thirteen this year."

"I better get him an archery set and teach him how to hunt with a bow and arrow," Curtis told her.

"That sounds like a good idea," she agreed.

Once at home, Curtis called his older brother and asked him if he would follow him tomorrow morning to the Diego place. He explained what he had in mind to do to Juan's house to further insulate it against the upcoming winter weather. Chance agreed to go and told Curtis he'd grab Woody too. With the three of them, it wouldn't take as long and they wouldn't be out in the cold as long either.

"See you in the morning then," Curtis said.

* * * * *

The next morning Chance and Woody arrived at Curtis's place early and helped him load the groceries for Juan Diego's family, putting part of them in Chance's vehicle.

Megan again had taken it upon herself to bake cookies for them. This time, they were peanut butter rather than the sugar cookies she had been baking for them. Her boys both liked her peanut cookies, so she hoped the Diego children would like them, too.

Ron Belcher had their box of frozen meat ready for them when they got to his place in Pueblo. Curtis Demming asked Belcher how much he owed him for the groceries he bought the Diego family awhile back.

"I had forgotten about that," Belcher laughed.

He looked up the bill and handed it to Curtis. After looking it over, Curtis pulled out his wallet and paid Belcher what they owed him, telling him he really appreciated Belcher doing that.

"We had ten inches of snow on the ground or I wouldn't have asked you to do it," Curtis told him.

"Anytime," Belcher replied. "You want me to go with you today? With all of us, we could make short work of what it looks like you guys are fixing to do."

"Sure, come on. You can ride with me," Curtis told him.

Juan came out of his house to greet them and helped them carry the groceries inside where Lucila began putting them up.

"Juan, we brought some insulation and some tarps to further insulate you house and hopefully keep you and your family warmer during the next few weeks," Curtis told him. "With you, that makes five of us, so it shouldn't take us long to get the job done."

Juan agreed and began helping to unload the rolls of insulation. Chance had brought several rolls of heavy masking tape, and they began by taping the end to the door jamb, then going around the house and cutting it at the other side of the door jamb and again applying masking tape. They were careful with the next row to make sure it was flush with the row below it. They then applied masking tape to the seams of the insulation. They did the same with the rest of the insulation.

At the top of the door, they had to cut part of the insulation to make room for the door to shut. Because he was the tallest, Chance got to do most of the roof by himself. They put his and his brother's pickups on either side of the house and stretched a ladder between them for him to work from, only having to move the vehicles twice for him to get it all done. Last were the tarps. They fitted the roof first with a tarp and worked from there, manipulating the tarps where they needed them and applying masking tape where it was needed to keep the wind from peeling the tarps from the building.

"I will leave the rest of this tape with you, Juan, just in case you need it. These strong winter winds could possibly cause it to come loose in places. I hope not, but just in case it does, you'll be able to tape it back," Chance told him.

"Gracias, Senors. You are too good to us. Come inside and get warm," he told them.

The men followed Juan inside and were surprised at how much warmer the house was already. After a few minutes, Woody suggested they go get Juan some wood to see him through for a while.

They took both pickups. Chance again found an area he could take the chain saw and made short work of tree trimming and cutting firewood in between cutting fallen trees the others had found for him to cut up. It took the better part of two hours to fill both pickup beds to capacity, after which they returned to the rough little house Juan and his family lived in. There they stacked their harvested wood to what Juan still had from the last time they had done this for him.

Juan asked them again to come in and warm up, but they declined, telling him they needed to get back to their own families. Juan shook hands with each of them and again expressed his thanks to them.

On the way back to Pueblo, Ron Belcher commented to Curtis Demming, "You and your brothers have been a Godsend to Juan and his family."

Curtis smiled and answered, "He will work it out when we start building corrals and buying livestock out at our Cabin place this summer. I think he will work out for us just like we have for him."

The wind had come up and brought colder air with it, and the sky was beginning to get overcast. Even the sun was debating whether or not to stay out any longer. It had been a cold and tiring afternoon. They were glad to be home again.

24

It was early April, and Curtis had his tax files ready to take to his accountant. He realized he had totally forgotten Taylor's birthday. Never before had he forgotten either of his son's birthdays. Hopefully, Taylor would forgive him. Lorne had a birthday coming up on the twenty-second. He would buy them both hunting vests to wear out in the country, especially during hunting season. It was hard to believe Taylor was already thirteen, and Lorne would soon be eleven.

He walked into the kitchen where Megan was mixing cake batter.

"Megan, guess what we both forgot?" he said.

Looking surprised, she asked him, "What?"

"Taylor's birthday," he told her as he reached for a cup to pour coffee into.

She stopped beating the cake batter, put a hand across her mouth, and exclaimed, "Oh, Curtis! How did we manage to forget that?"

"I don't know, Megan. Maybe we can get by with celebrating his birthday with Lorne's."

He walked down the hall to Taylor's room and knocked. Taylor told him to come in, surprised that his dad had come to his room.

"Taylor, son, your Mom and I completely forgot about your birthday. I wanted to apologize for forgetting. And if it's okay with you, we'll celebrate your birthday with Lorne's." he told his son.

Taylor got up from his chair in front of his computer.

He gave his Dad a hug and told him, "You know something, Dad? I forgot about it too!"

"You're just trying to make me feel better," his Dad replied.

"No, Dad. Honest. I did forget. I guess it's because we were all so concerned with that Diego family and trying to find out about those old graves out at the cabin, but I did forget, and celebrating with Lorne on his birthday will be great."

Curtis hugged Taylor then walked back to the kitchen where Megan was just then pouring the cake batter into nine-inch-by-thirteen-inch cake pan. He watched as she put it in the oven and turned on the timer.

He told her of his conversation with their newly turned teenager.

She smiled and said, "We'll have to make sure that is a special day for both of them."

"I'm sure Chance and Woody forgot too. I'll call them in a few minutes and remind them. They may want to do something special for their nephews too," he commented. "This may turn out to be Taylor and Lorne's best birthday ever!"

Curtis called his brothers and reminded them of Lorne's upcoming birthday, telling them that they were going to celebrate Taylor's birthday along with Lorne's on Lorne's birthday. He also told them what he planned to get the boys for their birthday gifts.

They too had forgotten Taylor's birthday but promised to be there for the double birthday for them.

"Why don't you come for supper tomorrow night?" he asked each of them.

They both accepted. It would be good to eat Megan's cooking again.

* * * * *

The next evening, Megan fixed fried chicken to go with their meal. She had not fixed fried chicken for some time, not since Chance had filled their freezers and the big locker in Pueblo with deer, ram, and elk meat. She fixed plenty, knowing there would be no leftover chicken and probably not much of the rest. And if they had room, there was still the cake she baked the day before.

When they had filled their plates, Curtis asked, "What would you guys think of us building a cabin out near ours and later moving

Juan Diego out there? He could help us build it and help build a couple of sheds and the corrals we want for the horses and mules."

Neither Chance nor Woody answered immediately.

"I like the idea, but first we best go out there and decide where we want to put each thing and then see about clearing the area we want to build on," Chance said at length.

"How large would you want to build their house?" Woody asked with concern in his voice.

"I figure with three kids, they will need at least three bedrooms—one for Luis and Mateo, one for Manuela, and one for Juan and Lucila. And like ours, theirs would need indoor water in the kitchen." Curtis replied.

"We need a shed to put the vehicles in when we're out there. We need a shed we can close to store grain in. And we need a shed for the horses and mules. We need a large corral and a round pen," Chance added.

"Well, we have plenty of timber," Woody stated. "This might turn into an all-summer job since we are all three working. I suggest building their cabin first and getting them moved out there rather than having to drive back and forth to Pueblo. In fact, if you two have no objections, we could allow them to stay in our cabin while we get theirs built."

"We also need to clear a space for Juan and Lucila to plant a garden," Curtis said.

"Let's go out this coming week end and see what they think of the idea."

Chance looked long at his brothers, and they waited for him to speak.

"Guys, I think it would be a good idea to move them on into our cabin if they will agree to it. I'll get my rifle and knives out of it, and, Woody, you get yours. There isn't much else they can get hurt with or destroy. I really don't know why we didn't move them before now."

"Probably because we really didn't know them that well. And because we've had that burial site on our minds. And because it is winter. I think we best go ahead and fence it. It may take several more months or even years before the Archaeologist can uncover some useful information about it," Woody stated.

"You want me to bring one of those big sheets of paper we use in the conference room at the tour center home with me so we can make a diagram of what we plan to do?" Woody asked. "We could take it with us and show it to Juan this weekend and see what he thinks about it. He may want his cabin built differently or in a different spot than we originally sketch it on the diagram or a different place for his garden."

"That sounds like a good idea, Woody," Chance told him, and Curtis agreed.

"And," Curtis added, "if he will agree to let us move him and his family into our cabin, until we can get one built for him, it would allow us to start building a lot sooner."

"Yeah, and we got a lot to do out there before we can even think about getting any animals," Woody commented.

"I think that settles it," Chance said.

He refilled their coffee cups and told his sister-in-law he would fix supper for them.

25

Two days later, after all three brothers got off work, they once again met at Curtis Demming's house where they borrowed the kitchen table to lay out the large blank sheet Woody had brought from the tour center, along with #2 pencils to sketch their layout for the cabin area of their land.

Chance thought the cabin they were going to build for the Diego's should be at least as far away from their own as a city block so as to give each family their own space. They would probably want their garden to the east to catch the morning sun, feasibly behind his cabin or to one side of it.

Woody contributed the south of where the cabins were to build the corral and round pen for the livestock they planned to buy. That left the grain shed to be built just north of the round pen to the west and also the shed to park the vehicles in and double as their tool shed on one end. It would be north of the grain shed not too far from their cabins. Curtis reminded them they needed to find water for both the corral and for Juan's cabin and a shed for the horses and mules to get in out of the weather also.

"You know, the boys can help some. Mateo should be able to help some, too. He's Lorne's age. They can do things like trim the small limbs from the trees we fell and pile them to one side. They should be able to pick rocks out of our way and pile them somewhere. And if we show them how to do it, they can help notch the logs for the buildings," Chance suggested.

Young ears had caught the sound of their uncle's voice, and now his nephews stood close by, listening. They both liked the idea of Mateo helping them help the men build the cabin area.

"Uncle Chance, what will we use to trim the little limbs with?" Taylor asked his Uncle.

"We'll get some hatchets and teach all three of you boys how to use them. We can teach you how to skin the logs out to build the buildings with, and we can teach you how to notch the logs. We'll have the tools for all of that for both you boys and us men to use. It will be good for all of you to learn. You might someday want to build your own cabin homes. We don't expect you boys to be able to do as much as us men do either. And there will be no need to rush because we want you to work safely. We don't need anybody hurt," Uncle Chance answered him.

"When are we gonna start?" Taylor prompted.

"We are going to talk to Juan about it first," his Dad told him. "And if he agrees to move into our cabin, then we can start within a few days after we get them moved. We three can only be out there on the weekends and on our days off. Until school is out, you two can only go out on the weekends too. But we can find enough for Juan and Mateo to do while we can't be there. And he may have Manuela and Luis pick up and move some of the smaller rocks that need moved. When school is out, we can all work more on getting things in order and getting them built."

"We're all off tomorrow, so let's make a trip to Pueblo in the morning," Chance suggested. "Juan shouldn't need more than a light load of groceries and a box of meat. We can pick those up on the way through Pueblo."

"Sounds good to me," Woody agreed.

Curtis added his own, "Me too."

* * * * *

When they reached the Diego place the next day, they were once again met by Juan Diego, who invited them in and helped them carry the groceries inside of his house, such as it was.

"Juan, we have a proposition we wanted to run by you and see what you think," Curtis told him.

"Let me hear what you have to say, Senors," Juan said to them, motioning for them to sit down.

"We want to know if you would be willing to move into our cabin out on our property west of Walsenburg until such time as we can get a cabin built out there for you and your family?" Curtis told him.

Juan Diego's face was a picture of total surprise. He had not once ever dreamed of getting such an offer as this. He lowered his head a few moments as tears of joy crept into his eyes.

"Senors, why would you do this for me and my family?" Juan asked.

All three of the Demming brothers smiled, and Chance's gentle voice told him, "Because we believe we can trust you, Juan. We told you before we will need your help to build sheds and corrals out there. But after talking it over, we decided it would be better for your family to live on the property. Our cabin is empty right now, so we can go ahead and move you folks into it for now. It's much better than what you have here and much closer to all of us as far as travel goes. Plus, when school is out, my two nephews and Mateo can help us. We will teach the boys what they need to know, and I'm sure there are things you can teach them too. Plus, there's plenty of room for you to have a nice garden out there."

"I don't know what to say, Senor," Juan told him.

"In that case, just say yes," Curtis told him.

Lucila walked over to her husband and put arm around his waist and looked up at him. He gave her a hug and spoke to her in Spanish, telling her what the Demming brothers had said to him. She had never shown emotions before, but now she walked over and gave each of the men a hug.

"I take it that means *yes*," Woody commented.

Juan nodded and hugged his wife to him.

"If you want, we can load those groceries into the bed of the truck and put Lucila and Juan and one of the kids in the front of the truck, and the other two kids in the back seat with Woody and Chance, and we can take you with us now. Then we can bring all three pickup trucks tomorrow and get the rest of your things. How does that sound?" Curtis asked.

Juan looked at Lucila and told her in Spanish what Curtis had just said. She smiled and nodded.

"While she gets the kids ready to go, let's get the groceries loaded and tied to the back of the truck," Curtis told Juan and his brothers.

When they got to the cabin, Cutis told them to stay in the vehicle while he got the fireplace going and some coffee going.

"Does anyone need to use the bathroom?" Woody asked.

The children all did, so he helped them out of the truck and took them around to the outhouse. Lucila and Juan followed. As soon as they were all finished, he took them back to the truck to get warmed up again. It would be a few minutes before the cabin would be warmed up.

As soon as Curtis waved at them, Woody took the Diego family to the cabin and then helped Chance get the groceries and the things Juan's family had brought with them inside.

Curtis showed Juan and Lucila through the house, showing them where the beds and cots were, where the linen closet was, where the pantry was, and he showed Lucila how the water worked in kitchen sink. He showed Juan where the wood box was and where they kept the few tools, including the ax he and his brothers had used to cut the wood for both the cookstove and the fireplace.

"This will be better for you," he said. "You won't have to walk half a mile to the river to bring back water. And I think there's enough wood already cut to last you a while. If not, it's not that far to walk to find wood. You will be much warmer here and not as apt to catch colds."

"Senors, how can we ever thank you?" Juan asked.

Chance put an arm around Juan's shoulders and told him, "You can thank us by saying you'll help us. In a few days, we can start bringing in the timbers to build you your own cabin. And as soon as we can, we'll get yours built for you. Meantime, we still have some really bad weather coming in, and we'd all feel a lot better knowing you and your family are in our cabin staying warm instead of us wondering if you're warm enough over there at Pueblo."

He took his arm from around Juan, continuing to explain that once they got Juan's cabin built, Juan could stake out a garden plot wherever he and his wife wanted it, and they would—if they needed to—adjust their plans for building the corrals and sheds.

He stopped talking and looked at Lucila and the children.

"Do you think you will like it here?" he asked them.

Juan translated in Spanish. Lucila smiled and nodded, and their children followed their mother's example.

"I guess we better show her where we keep the dishes and eating utensils," Woody said.

"That's a good idea," Curtis told him. "Lucila might want to fix them a bite to eat after a while."

After Woody showed Lucila where those items were, he told them he and his brothers would come get Juan in the morning and would pick up all three of their vehicles in Walsenburg and get the rest of their things moved to the cabin for them.

"Meantime, you guys make yourselves at home," Curtis told them. "This is still out in the middle of nowhere, but at least you will be able to stay warm. And we've got some bad weather coming."

Juan Diego shook all three brothers' hands and again thanked them for all they were doing for him and his family.

26

Curtis Demming went to the cabin the next morning to pick up Juan Diego.

He told Juan as he got into the truck, "Chance and Woody are meeting us at my place in town, and we will go to Pueblo from there."

Juan nodded in acknowledgement.

"Do you think you and your family are going to like living at the cabin, Juan?" he asked.

"Si, Senor. It is beautiful out there, and the cabin is so much warmer than the little house at Pueblo. Plus, Lucila loves the cookstove to cook on and also that there is water at the kitchen sink so she doesn't have to heat ice or snow to use in her cooking or for us to bathe in," Juan Diego replied.

"Well, let's get you moved. We can figure out what we want to do next," Curtis said as he pulled into his driveway where both of his brothers were waiting with their vehicles.

They arrived two hours later at the place where the Diego family had been living.

The containers they had brought to put thing in came in handy. They were able to put most of the clothing into one container. Another was used for the bedding, The others were used for cookware and dishes, and the rest were used for the leftover groceries Lucila had not formerly used.

The rest were the table and chairs and the bed the Diego's had of their own. And last but not to be left behind was the elk hide that could be used again later in Juan's new cabin once they got it built.

"I'm going to stop at the Meat Processing Plant," Curtis told his brothers. "I know Megan needs some meat, and I'm pretty sure we need to fill the cooler for Lucila too. So you two go on and Juan and I will meet you at the cabin."

"Sounds like a plan," Chance said, as he and Woody headed back toward Walsenburg and their cabin.

Ron Belcher was glad to see Curtis and Juan.

"Good to see you two!" he exclaimed. "How've you been, Juan? How are your children?"

"I need to pick up a couple of large boxes of meat," Curtis told him. "We have moved him and his family out to our cabin. It's warmer out there, and we still have some bad weather in the forecast."

"How about that? I won't get to visit you as often, Juan. But I think God was smiling on you the day these Demming brothers took you and your family under their wing."

"When the weather clears up, we'll build him a cabin of his own out there. But until then, they can use ours. You can come visit them any time, Belcher," Curtis told him. "In fact, if you can drum up some spare time later on, you can come out and help us put their cabin together."

Ron Belcher nodded and told Curtis, "Let me know when. You have my phone number."

Curtis assured Belcher he would call him when they started on Juan's cabin. He and Juan shook hands with Belcher then headed back toward Walsenburg. By the time they reached the cabin, Chance and Woody had unloaded their trucks and were waiting on their brother and Juan Diego to arrive.

As they got out of the truck and began to unload, Curtis told them Belcher had said to call him when they started to build Juan's cabin. Both said okay. Curtis carried one box of meat to the cooler they had used previously, opened it, put the packages of meat inside, and closed it again, telling Juan that cooler was what he and his brothers had used last fall to keep the meat frozen.

"And after the snow fell, we made snowballs and let them freeze, then used them in the cooler around the meat to help keep it frozen," Curtis added.

"Juan, I know we moved you from the middle of nowhere over at Pueblo to the middle of nowhere west of Walsenburg, but at least here you will be warm and you have plenty of food for a while. And we can check with you more often," Chance told him. "So you take care of yourself and your family. You might think of where you want your cabin built and also where you want your garden and flowerbeds. We need to be getting back, so we'll see you later."

"Senors, thank you again. We will be fine here, and we truly appreciate that you men have done so much for us already," Juan said as he shook hands with all of them.

* * * * *

The three Demming brothers once again met at Curtis's house. Megan had supper cooked and ready for them.

"How did it go today?" she asked them.

"I think it went well," her husband answered her. "We got the rest of Juan and Lucila's things moved. Ron Belcher offered to help build their cabin when we can start on it. I stopped and picked up a box of meat for them, and I brought a box home for our freezer too."

"Good," she said.

Then turning to her brother-in-law Woody, Megan said, "Woody, you need to call Paul Dunhurst in the morning."

"Right. Maybe they've found something out," he replied.

"I sure hope so," Curtis commented.

Chance voiced a thought that had just came to him. "I wonder if those old graves could be something other than Indian graves."

"What do you mean, Chance?" Woody asked.

"I was thinking that maybe when the Mormons moved from Nebraska to Utah—if they may have crossed Colorado to get there— that would have been in the mid-1800s and about the same era of time that Cholera outbreaks were affecting people. If that were the case, those who survived it would have buried the rest and went on to Utah."

"What's Cholera, Uncle Chance?" Taylor asked.

"It's a serious bacterial infection of the small intestines that people get from drinking contaminated water, and back then, folks were in the habit of drinking from rivers and streams or anywhere they found water during their travels. It affects people with severe fever, vomiting, and dysentery," his uncle explained to him.

"What's dysentery?" his nephew wanted to know.

"It's a disease that causes uncontrollable diarrhea, filled with blood and mucus in the bowel movements, and is commonly associated with Cholera victims. The victims usually suffer a lot of pain," Uncle Chance told him. "Most people die from it."

"But if there were survivors," Woody elaborated on his brother's thoughts, "that might account for those old wagon tracks that run to the burial ground. The survivors would have buried their dead and went on to Utah or wherever they were going."

"But wouldn't they have reported the graves?" Lorne asked.

"Not necessarily. During that era of time, not many people crossing the Plains area reported burial places. Either they didn't know where to report them or just didn't remember to do it," Chance remarked.

"It could have also been a wagon train headed for California with White settlers too," Curtis put in. "Although I doubt if settlers would have built stone mounds over the graves. They may have in an attempt to keep the disease from spreading."

"I will run those ideas by Dunhurst in the morning," Woody told them.

"Let us know what he says," Curtis told him.

"I will," Woody said.

27

Woody called Paul Dunhurst early the next morning and got a buzzing sound indicating his line was busy. He made himself some coffee and breakfast and then tried again. When Paul Dunhurst answered, Woody told him who he was and that he was returning Dunhurst's call from the day before.

"Yes, Mr. Demming," Dunhurst said. "I called to let you know Mr. Krigler was unable to get State permits to exhume one of the graves on your property."

"How come?" Woody asked him.

"It seems like that from the photos he took and submitted with the application, the State Officials decided the graves were too old to be looked into further," Dunhurst told him.

"Well, let me run this by you then. My brothers and I were talking last night about the possibility that those might be Mormon graves from when the Mormons migrated from Nebraska to Utah," Woody told him.

"I will certainly mention that to Krigler," Dunhurst replied.

"The other thing one of my brothers mentioned is could it be possible those were from a White wagon train who may have been victims of the Cholera epidemic and perhaps put the stones over their dead to keep the disease from spreading? You know there's still ruts out there on that old road showing some type of wagons traveled that area," Woody explained to Dunhurst.

"That's another interesting concept. I'll mention it to Charles Krigler also. And if it's okay, can we come out to your place again and take another look at those graves?" Dunhurst responded.

"Certainly. Any time you want to, Mr. Dunhurst. Just give us a call and let us know when you'll be here," Woody told the Archaeology Professor.

"Thank you, Mr. Demming. I will talk to Krigler and let you know something as soon as I can," Paul Dunhurst assured him.

After he hung up from talking to Professor Dunhurst, Woody called each of his two brothers and told them what Dunhurst had told him, including that Dunhurst wanted to come out and look at the grave site again and wanted to bring Charles Krigler with him.

"That sounds like a good idea," Curtis told him. "Maybe that will let them find something they over looked the first time. Did he say when he wanted to come out?"

"No, but he is supposed to call us before they come," Woody told him.

"Well then, Woody, I think we need to start felling trees and getting ready to build Juan's cabin as soon as we can," Curtis replied.

Woody agreed. They were both sure Chance would agree also.

* * * * *

Three days later, they gathered the tools they would need, including purchasing some extra log chains and debarking tools and hatchets. If all went well that day, they would be able to cut and drag felled and trimmed trees from the east side of their property.

Juan Diego met them as they got out of their vehicles. Curtis told him of their plans to start felling trees and dragging home poles for building his cabin.

"Have you decided where you want it?" Curtis asked.

"Si, Senor. We think it would be good to build it here," he said, walking to an area some three hundred yards from the Demming cabin. "Lucila wanted to plant the garden about thirty feet on east of the house, and if it is okay, she wants to plant an area about fifty by a hundred feet."

"I don't see any reason she can't have a garden that size or even larger, Juan," Chance told him. "How big do you want your cabin to be? Maybe three bedrooms? That would let the boys have their own bedroom and Manuela her own, although hers could be a little smaller than theirs. And then you will need one for you and Lucila. Then you will need a kitchen and a living room at least as big as ours."

"That sounds good, Senor Chance," Juan told him.

"Okay, then. Go tell Lucila where we are going and that we may not be back for several hours," Chance told him.

He retrieved his chainsaw from his vehicle while Curtis and Woody gathered what they would need.

"Let's leave the vehicles here for now," Woody suggested.

They all agreed because right now they wanted to fell and trim the trees for the logs they wanted to use. So there was no sense in having vehicles around that might get damaged by the falling trees. Plus, they might need to clear a roadway on which to get their vehicles to the trees they felled.

They walked for nearly half a mile before Chance saw the first tree he chose to test his chainsaw on. The other three stayed back out of the way until it landed on the ground where they could then use hatchets to trim the limbs from it and pile them to one side. One by one Chance found trees to cut, and the other three trimmed them as soon as they fell.

By late afternoon, they had felled and trimmed quite a few trees. Curtis mentioned bringing his truck down with the log chains so they could drag the trees closer to the cabin area. They were all in agreement, and on their way back, they picked up rocks and threw them out of the way and used the hatchets to break up dirt to fill in ruts that might damage the pickup. By the time they got to Curtis's truck, they had a road-like trail he would be able to get his pickup down into the canyon to get to the logs.

"Let's see if Lucila has some coffee made," Juan suggested.

She did, and they all enjoyed a cup while they rested. Juan filled her in on their afternoon progress and what they were going to do next. She smiled and said something to him in Spanish.

"She wants to know if you men are staying for supper," Juan told them.

"No," Curtis answered him. "Megan will have our supper waiting when we get home."

Juan translated that to his wife.

Curtis backed his vehicle around and drove carefully to the end of the canyon to tie on the last log. Chance, however, cut that log in half and tied it with one of the chains and had Curtis pull forward to the next log. He did it the same way tying these two to the first two after the fashion of a raft. After that, he began stacking logs on top of those four, careful not to overload his brother's pickup. Curtis dragged the logs to the cabin area, and they unloaded where Juan had indicated they should stack the logs. Next they took Woody's vehicle and loaded it the same way to bring logs home. They used Chance's vehicle last.

It was nearing dark when they unloaded Chance's pickup. They decided to quit for the day and go home. They shook hands with Juan Diego and told him thanks for his help with the trees and the logs.

Woody and Chance both stopped at their brother's house. They knew Megan would have supper ready for them, and they were hungry.

"Who do you know that drills wells?" Curtis asked his brothers.

The question caught them off guard. They looked at him a few minutes before either answered.

"Why?" it was Chance who asked.

"Because if Juan and Lucila are going to have indoor water in their kitchen like we have in our cabin, don't you think we need a well drilled? Or had you planned to dig it by hand?" Curtis asked with a bit of sarcasm in his voice.

Woody put his fork down and replied, "I think maybe Marvin Hodges does well drilling. I'll ask him."

"We need to see about getting that done before we build their cabin," Curtis said. "I'd rather not have to tear out part of the cabin to get that done after we build it."

Chance uttered a low laugh. "That does make sense, Curtis. Besides, we may have to change the location of their cabin to accommodate the underground water reservoir. We have a good water supply in our cabin, but two hundred yards east where Juan wants to build his cabin, there might not be as much of a water supply."

"Why not, Uncle Chance?" Lorne asked.

"Because the underground stream may not be wide enough to reach that far. It will be nice if it does, but it may not. And if it doesn't, then we will have to find a spot that does have a good supply of water, even if Juan has to change locations of his cabin and let us build it directly south of ours. We know we have a sufficient water supply, and if we have to drill into the same supply for Juan, then at least we will know they have a good supply of water also," Chance explained to his nephew.

"But won't that run us out of water at our cabin?" Taylor asked him.

Chance smiled and answered, "No, Taylor. We have plenty of water. It will last a long time unless the ground shifts somewhere down below and cuts the stream off."

"Why would it do that?" Lorne wanted to know.

"Sometimes the ground underneath shifts for various reasons. Could be caused from a small earthquake that causes the ground underneath to shift. Or I suppose there are other things that could cause it to shift," Chance answered.

His nephews were getting into a topic he knew little about. But kids were good at that. They could put a person in a spot with some of their questions, and they fully expected adults to know the answers they sought. His brother Woody came to his rescue.

"Let's call it a night," Woody suggested. "I'll see what I can come up with tomorrow."

28

Woody looked up the number for Marvin Hodges the next morning. When the man answered, Woody explained to him about needing a well drilled on their property west of Walsenburg for a cabin they were intending to build and asked if Mr. Hodges could do that for them. Woody also asked when Mr. Hodges would be available to go with them to look at the project.

"Mr. Demming," Marvin Hodges said. "I haven't done that kind of well digging in several years, but I will certainly come out and take a look at what you want done. Then if I don't feel I can do it, I may know someone who can."

"When would you be able to look at it?" Woody asked him.

"Would this Tuesday around two in the afternoon work for you?" Hodges asked.

"We'll make it work. Can we meet you at the gas station on the north side of town?" Woody responded.

Sounds good to me. I may bring my son along too. He's pretty good with plumbing and such," Hodges replied.

"Good. We will see you then," Woody said.

He called Chance and Curtis, telling both they may have to take off work Tuesday afternoon so they too could be on hand to meet Marvin Hodges and his son. They could also be on hand to listen to what Hodges and his son told them about getting a water well drilled for Juan's cabin. They both agreed. He himself would have to take off from work Tuesday afternoon in order to be there.

They met Hodges and his son, Calvin, at the gas station Tuesday afternoon and had Hodges follow them out to their cabin. There they introduced Juan to them and explained that they wanted to have water inside the cabin they were fixing to build for Juan Diego. That day was warmer by several degrees than the previous days had been.

"Can I have a look inside at how the water in this cabin is set up?" Marvin Hodges asked them.

As they entered the cabin, Curtis introduced Lucila to the Hodges, and Juan translated for her. She smiled and stepped back out of the way.

Marvin Hodges was about five feet ten inches tall and carried a little extra weight beneath his graying head of hair. Young Calvin Hodges was an inch taller than his dad but slender with light red hair and blue eyes.

Marvin Hodges wore overalls and now pulled a tape measure out of his pocket and a small notepad and an ink pen. Kneeling down in front of the indoor pump, he began measuring the pipe and connections, writing down the measurements as he went. He checked the information on the pump for size and manufacturer information and date it was installed. Then he measured from the pipe to the cabin wall and the height from the floor to the top of the cabinet in which the sink was installed, measuring also the length and width of the countertop itself.

He stood up and checked the information he had written down on his writing pad and returned it and the ink pen and tape measure to his pockets. He then tried the water spout and was satisfied with the flow of water it poured into the sink.

"Now," he asked, "where did you want to build the other cabin?"

Curtis noticed that as Calvin Hodges followed his dad out of the house, he was counting his steps. Once outside, he walked the same number of steps back along the cabin wall and stopped.

"Can someone hand me a fair-sized rock?" he asked.

Woody Demming was standing by a tan-colored rock. He picked it up and walked over to Calvin Hodges and handed the rock to him. The younger man immediately placed the rock where the end of his boot indicated the place where the indoor faucet was in the kitchen inside the cabin, giving them a marker to work from.

"Thanks," Calvin said. "Now how far out do you guys intend to build the second cabin?"

Woody told him, and again Calvin Hodges counted his steps as he stepped off the three hundred yards from the cabin to where the second one would be built. He stopped and asked which way the kitchen would be facing.

They looked to Juan Diego for the answer. He thought a few minutes, looking back at the cabin and again at where Calvin Hodges was now standing. The current cabin kitchen area faced the south. Coming straight across to the new cabin, the kitchen could face any of the other three directions, but finally Juan chose the east. The wind and storms came across mostly from the north and west so he reasoned the cabin would be warmer if the kitchen faced the east. The sink could be at the far northern corner of it so that the waterline would be in line with the older cabin.

Juan took it on himself to draw a diagram on the ground with a stick of how they would design the kitchen and told them, "I think this would be the best way to build it, Senors."

Again Woody handed Calvin a fairly large rock to mark the place where he and his father would drill the well for Juan's kitchen.

"We can start on this Saturday if that is okay with the rest of you," Marvin Hodges told them.

They all agreed, including Juan Diego.

"They seem to know what they're doing," Curtis said as he and his brothers watch the Hodges men start back toward Walsenburg.

"While we are waiting for them to bring the water line into the cabin, why don't we start clearing the areas on which we want to build the corrals and maybe getting one of them built?"

They walked to the south, leaving ample room for the new cabin and play area for the kids. Chance picked up two lengths of tree limbs that were nearly the same size. With his knife, he quickly removed the limbs from them. When they stopped, he crossed the limbs to form an *X*, then found four rocks and placed them at the intersection of the limbs.

"What's that for?" Curtis asked.

Chance laughed and asked his youngest brother, "Haven't you ever heard that '*X* marks the spot'?"

"Oh. I forgot," Curtis admitted.

"Well, let's get back to town before Megan disowns us," Chance said.

"And where we will be walking encyclopedias for our nephews," Woody added.

"Senors, do you want me to start working on the corrals?" Juan asked them.

"You know, that's a good idea, Juan," Curtis answered him. "You and Mateo can measure how large you want them, then lay them out with limbs for now. That will give us an outline to set the posts by later on."

Juan smiled and told him okay.

* * * * *

Chance went back out to the cabin when he got off work the next day. He took along his chainsaw, a couple of hatchets, and two logging chains. He found Juan and Mateo laying out a corral with fallen tree limbs.

"Juan, let's go ahead and start laying posts where we want them. I'll cut the trees we felled the other day into posts. I'm going to cut them in eight-foot lengths, and you two can lay them ten feet apart. We'll leave room to drag other felled trees from the south range through the corral for the cabin," he told his newfound friend. "We still have about three hours of good light, so we can maybe get most of the first corral laid out. Then tomorrow I'll bring my post hole diggers and we can get some of the posts set."

"I'll have Mateo and Manuela pick the rocks up out of the corral area and stack them to one corner," Juan told him.

"Good deal. And when we skin out the posts, save the bark for the fireplace," Chance commented.

He got his chainsaw from his pickup, along with a measuring tape with which he measured the logs. He marked them with a nail he carried in his pocket. Then he commenced to cut them into posts which Juan and his son Mateo carried to the corral and spaced them at the intervals Chance had told Juan a few minutes ago. Mateo could only pick up one end of a post, so he was forced to drag the other end. He seemed proud to be helping his father. He worked tirelessly with the energy of youth, and not once did he complain. Chance was proud of him, and he knew Juan was proud of him too.

By the time Chance ran out of posts to cut, they still had forty-five minutes of good daylight left. But they had gotten a lot done, and he knew young Mateo was tired, although he would not admit it in front of Chance. Chance gave Mateo a hug and shook hands with Juan before he left.

* * * * *

The next afternoon, Chance again went to the cabin. This time, he took his post hole digger and a couple of the debarking tools with which to skin the posts. He later helped Juan skin out the posts he had cut the day before and had Mateo take the bark pieces to the cabin to be used in the fireplace. Then he left Juan to dig postholes while he went to the south and cut more trees to cut for posts. Then he trimmed them and cut them into posts which he stacked into the bed of his pickup.

By the time he got back to the corral, Juan had several posts set on one side of the corral. They looked good. He was proud of what Juan and Mateo had done. He had Juan help him unload his pickup, then showed Juan how to use the debarking tool, which made skinning the posts both easier and faster.

"I probably won't be back until Saturday. Have Lucila make a list of what she needs from town, and I'll bring them with me Saturday," he told Juan.

Juan said nothing but quickly disappeared into the cabin. Moments later, he handed Chance a list he had written in English. Chance thanked him, smiled, and got into his pickup and headed home. He was proud of what the Mexican and his son had accomplished and proud too that he and his brothers had helped them through the winter.

29

Saturday promised to be a busy day all around. Marvin Hodges and his son Calvin arrived with the tools and equipment they needed to get a well drilled for the new cabin.

The Demming brothers felled trees and removed the limbs for the sides of the cabin and dragged them close to where they needed them for the cabin. Woody suggested they search the west and northern areas and see if they could fell some of the lodge pole trees from those areas. They could be used for the long sides of the cabin and perhaps the roof also. Their three pickups were never tiring workhorses, and by late evening, they had a good-sized stack of long lodge pole logs at the cabin area.

Even Marvin Hodges commented, "You guys did good."

"We should be able to start building the cabin this week," Curtis said. "By tomorrow, we should have enough logs brought in to get most of it done anyway. Then if we need more, we can go cut some more."

"Calvin and I can come out and help put it up tomorrow. Or at least get it started, if you want us to," Marvin Hodges offered.

"That would be great," Chance told him. "With all of us working on it, we can get it done quicker. And what we have left to do when we quit tomorrow evening, we can work on as we can."

"All right, we'll see you in the morning then. We'll need to bring some ladders too. I think I may have an extension ladder somewhere. I'll see if I can find it and I'll bring it with us," Marvin Hodges told them.

He and his son shook hands all around before leaving.

"I didn't think to ask him what we owe him for putting that well in," Curtis stated.

"We can let them help put up this new cabin and then ask him what we owe him. We will surely need to pay for him and his son helping us put up the cabin," Woody told him.

"Chance, if you want, I can see about working half days this week and you and I can work on this in the afternoons after you get off work," Woody said to his older brother.

He knew Curtis could not get off early from his job. But he and Chance and Juan could do a lot toward finishing the new cabin during the afternoons.

"Okay," Chance replied. "Sounds like a good idea if the weather holds. We can make a lot of headway."

"Why don't I bring my table saw tomorrow? I can leave it here for you two to use for trimming out the frames for the windows. I'm sure Lucila will want some windows put in," Curtis suggested.

"Maybe we better ask her what size windows she wants and how many," Chance said. "We might want to stop at the Lumber Yard and see if they have the size she wants. We also need to see about getting doors. At least three for the bedrooms and two for going in and out of the house."

"Woody can you do a drawing of how the house is going to be? You can then put a box for the windows and a forward slash for the doors. Bring it with you tomorrow, and we will let Lucila and Juan look it over. If they want something moved, then move it. It will be much easier to move on paper before we start building. When she and Juan get it to their specifications, then write down the size of the windows she wants put in. Those may need to wait for a week day so we can get them ordered. But we can still build and insert the frames into the log structure," Chance explained.

"Depending on how much we get done tomorrow, we may have this cabin done by this time next week," Curtis commented. "You'd like that, wouldn't you, Juan?"

Juan smiled and answered, "Si, Senor."

"We'll still have to build closets and a pantry and kitchen cabinets and shelves. But those are things you can do, Juan, once we get the house finished. Some of those rocks the kids have put in piles can be used to build the fireplace and the chimney. I guess I better stop by the Mercantile on the way home and pick up some cement and a bucket or two and maybe a couple of trowels," Curtis said.

"We better be going then," Woody told him. "We'll see you in the morning, Juan."

"Building the fireplace took a lot longer than any of them had planned. They used the larger rocks to build the floor and lower walls, inserting a length of left over pipe, to which they welded iron hooks, to use for hanging kettles on when ever Lucila decided to cook at the fireplace. They pieced together a shelf above the fireplace and smoothed it level to use as a mantelpiece, then used the smaller rocks to build the chimney. It wasn't the prettiest chimney ever built, but it worked. And at that time, a working chimney was a blessing, no matter how drab it may look.

Before any of them left, they brought in some small pieces of the logs and built the first fire in it to make sure it worked like it was built to work. Much to their satisfaction, it did. They let the fire burn itself out before they left for the evening. The cement would take a couple of days at least to fully dry. By then, it would be ready for everyday use.

While the cement dried on the fireplace they could work on the other sheds and corrals and figure out where to also build an outhouse near the cabin they were finishing for the Diego family.

Satisfied his brothers would get a goodly amount of work done during the next two days, Curtis decided to go on home. They would more than likely get the roof done in his absence, he figured. He planned to spend the rest of the day with his own family.

* * * * *

Megan had taken fresh-baked cookies out of the oven. She handed a small plate of them to her husband, along with a cup of coffee, when he came into the kitchen. He sat them both on the counter and pulled her into his arms and kissed her.

"I love you, Megan," he told her.

She smiled and said, "I know that, and I love you too. How's the new cabin coming along?"

"It's gettin' there. Chance and Woody are going out tomorrow and Tuesday afternoons. They will most likely get the roof done or at least get it started. Then we'll be ready to start on building the closets and such and getting Juan moved in. I figure we have about a week left before it will be completely finished," he told her.

"Good deal. Maybe me and the boys can go out with you this coming weekend and see it," she responded.

He picked up his coffee and tasted a cookie before telling her, "That's a date, lady."

She smiled again and laughed.

Curtis felt good to hear her laugh. It had been several weeks since he had heard her laugh.

"Where are the boys?" he asked.

"They went down to the ballpark with some of their friends to practice some baseball," she said. "They'll be back after a while."

On Thursday morning, just as Curtis picked up his jacket and started out the door for work, the phone rang. He answered it. His brother Woody informed him Professor Dunhurst had called and wanted to know if he and Charles Krigler could come out Saturday morning to view the grave site again.

"What did you tell him?" Curtis asked.

"I told him as far as I knew, it would be okay and to meet us at the gas station where we met them last time," Woody answered.

"Okay. How much did you and Chance get done on Juan's cabin this week?"

"We got the roof on it. Juan was going to see about building some cabinets and some closets for it. You know, Curtis, I'm glad we found him and his family. They seem to be really good people."

"They do, for a fact. Call Chance and let him know about Dunhurst and Krigler. I need to get to work," Curtis told his brother.

He was glad Woody had called him and glad to know that his brothers and Juan had gotten the roof put on the cabin. From the sound of what Woody had told him, the only things lacking were the doors to the outside and the windows. He had the measurements for the windows in his wallet. He could pick those up Friday morning and deliver them Saturday.

Juan, he reasoned to himself, may have the doors made by the time they got there Saturday. Juan had proved to be good with the table saw and a fair hand at carpentry as well.

30

The Demming brothers met Professor Dunhurst and State Archaeologist Charles Krigler at the gas station Saturday morning and had them follow them out to the cabins.

Once there, they introduced them to Juan.

"Wow! You have a new cabin built! That's nice!" Dunhurst stated.

"We built this one for Juan. He is now a part of our family and will be keeping an eye on things out here for us," Curtis told them. "Today he will go with us to that burial ground. We haven't told him of it, so he hasn't seen it yet. We will ride out there with my brothers. My truck has windows in it for this new cabin."

Chance elected to take his vehicle, so his brothers and Juan rode with him. As they rode, the brothers told Juan Diego about the burial site and brought him up-to-date on what had been done so far, told him that they planned to fence it later, and that they did not want any of the kids in it for any reason. They told him about Taylor and Lorne wanting to look for rocks for their rock collections and that they had explained that it was like the White people's cemeteries and completely off limits to them.

They all got out of the vehicles near the grave site. Krigler brought out a high-powered camera and began taking photos of it—at times, going to the backside of a grave for his photos. He adjusted his camera for closeup shots of some of the mounds and for long-range shots here and there also as he walked around the burial site.

The sun made it hard to get some of the photos Charles Krigler would like to have taken, but he took a lot where the sun allowed him to get good pictures.

The sky was clear, and the eagle spotted them. He flew low, scolding them for invading his domain. He made several low fights overhead before landing in the nearest tree to watch what the humans were doing.

Juan's curiosity got the best of him and finally he asked, "How did you guys find this burial site?"

"We were walking and looking at this land we purchased. One of those walks brought us to this old road," Curtis said, pointing the road out to Juan. "Chance saw it before the rest of us. He and Woody were ahead of me and Megan. My boys were with their uncles, and they had to be called back because they wanted to rummage through the mounds for rocks for the rock collections they have started. Being youngsters, they didn't know the rock mounds were graves. Or why we wouldn't let them dig through them. That will go for your children also. So we are going to fence it as soon as we can. We just have to wait for Mr. Krigler to do what he needs to do first."

"I see, Senor," Juan replied.

"Have you ever seen graves like these, Juan?" Woody asked.

Juan looked thoughtful for several minutes before he answered.

"A long time ago when I was little and my parents had hired out to a man down in Texas, I remember one graveyard where the graves were covered with stones, much like these are. They were called cairns and were very old, even back then. I do not know the history about them."

"Do you remember where in Texas your parents lived?" Woody asked.

"No, Senor, I am sorry. I was very little at the time. It seems like it was a long way down in Texas, but I do not remember where," Juan answered truthfully.

Archaeologist Charles Krigler overheard the conversation between Juan Diego and Woody Demming. He did not consider the possibility of this burial site on the Demming property as being a prehistoric site or the possibility that it was not on records in Colorado because Colorado was under the impression that no such burial sites existed in their State. And as far back on the property, as it was, it was possible that former owners had not walked the property as the Demmings had. To him, that would account for the burial site having not been found before the Demmings had discovered it on their property.

"The State had neither knowledge of it nor any records of it," Krigler told them. "That's what they based their denial for a permit to excavate on. They just do not want to believe it exists."

"You showed them the photos you took of it, didn't you?" Curtis asked him.

"Yes I did, but that didn't seem to matter. Even if they had accepted my report and photos, the State of Colorado does not allow DNA testing. Any remains we could find would have to be sent to Arizona or somewhere else to have the DNA tests done, which in itself could get expensive," he explained to them. "On top of that, the cost for having that done—in case we could get a permit to excavate one of the graves—would have to come from you men. The State of Colorado will not pay having it done."

"Then it looks like the only thing we can do is put a fence around it to keep the wildlife and the kids out," Chance commented.

"I will write out another report and add the photos I took today and file it in my office. But there's not much chance that it will go any further. I also intend to check into the old cairns Mr. Diego spoke of. Perhaps I can turn up some information about those that may relate to these," Krigler added. "And if it's okay with you folks, I would like to come visit from time to time to visit both you folks and this beautiful scenery."

"So would I," Paul Dunhurst said. "I want to see what you guys are going to do with the place now that you have a new cabin nearly finished and a corral already built. What do you aim to do with the corral?"

"We want to buy some mules and horses and maybe some donkeys to train to ride and also for pack animals. We thought we might be able to sell some along to those folk who are still hard scrabble miners who like to walk or ride to the areas they mine. Some of those places are high enough up in the mountains that you can't get a vehicle up to them," Curtis answered him. "We still have to build barns and sheds and a couple more corrals first."

"Wow! Sounds like a lot of work. We'll sure want to see it when you get done with everything," Dunhurst told him.

"I'm sure we all want to see it when we get it done. Later after we get the corrals finished, we'll have to have a well drilled for at least one of them. And then Juan and his wife want to plant a garden, and that will give the kids something to do to clear the garden area. So, yeah, there's plenty of work yet to be done," Curtis assured them.

They shook hands all around before Dunhurst and Krigler left.

"Sounds like the State Archaeologist got nowhere fast," Chance commented.

"Meantime, guys, let's get back to the cabins and get those windows put in and see what else we can get done," Woody said.

His tone of voice told his brothers he was highly disappointed that the Archaeologist had run into a dead end on the burial site. They felt disappointment too. But they said nothing as they climbed into Chance's pickup to go back to the cabins.

It was nearing dark when they finished putting in the last window. And looking over their work, they decided it looked rather nice. The closets and cabinets Juan had built so far were also nice. The only thing left to do was to make and hang the two doors. Curtis thought to pick up doorknobs for each door and the hinges for them when he had bought the materials for the windows. These he left with Juan before leaving for the evening.

"Megan and the boys will be with me tomorrow, Juan. Megan wants to see your new cabin," Curtis told Juan.

Juan's eyes sparkled. "It will be good to see Senora Demming again."

"It will be a good day for the kids to get better acquainted too," Curtis replied. "See you tomorrow."

* * * * *

That evening over supper, Curtis told his wife and boys what Paul Dunhurst and Charles Krigler had told the men folk that day at the burial site. He also told them he thought Krigler intended to do some further research about those graves, especially where Juan had remembered a burial ground much like that one when he was small and his people had worked on a place way down in Texas.

"We're going to go ahead and fence it when we get through with the cabin and the corrals. And we've already told Juan the kids are not to go near it," he finished.

Taylor and Lorne looked at each other remembering what their Uncle Chance had told them the day they found the burial ground on their property. They looked at their dad and nodded as if to tell him "okay."

"We're going out there tomorrow and let you guys see the cabin we built for Juan and Lucila and their family. And you boys can get better acquainted with Mateo and Luis and Manuela," he told them.

"Yeah!" they exclaimed in unison.

It had been some time since they had been able to go to the country, and they were excited at getting to go again.

"Mind you, Juan's family are still using our cabin. But maybe we can help them get moved into their own while we're there. Which reminds me, Megan, do you have any old curtains you can let Lucila use for a while until she can get some of her own?"

"I still have the box of them I took down from in here when we first moved in. I'll take those out to her," Megan replied.

"And if we have at least one spare lantern, we'll take that too," Curtis said. "We may have to let them use the cots also for the kids' bedrooms. They have their bed from the shanty at Pueblo. So they are okay, but the kids need somewhere to sleep besides the floor."

31

It was nearing noon when Curtis Demming and his family arrived at the cabins.

Lucila came over and gave Megan a hug and a smile, then motioned for Megan to follow her to the new cabin. Once inside, Megan Demming looked around admiringly. Juan had put the doors up the night before, and he had done an amazing job with the cabinets and closets. Lucila showed Megan the bedrooms also—the smaller one for Manuela, the next for the boys, which was a little larger, and the Master bedroom for herself and Juan.

"Nice!" Megan smiled at Lucilla.

They had moved their bed from the other cabin that morning and had begun moving the kitchen items into the new cabin also. They still had to move clothing and the food items.

Juan and Curtis came in, along with the boys and Manuela. Juan showed them through the cabin too, amid admiring glances and comments.

"You've done a good job, Juan," Curtis told him. "Let's get the rest of your things moved. Then we'll move the cots over for the kids to sleep on."

All of them went to the other cabin and began picking up items to transport to the new cabin. The groceries took the longest because they had not thought to bring any containers to put them in to take them across to the new cabin. When the last of their things had been transferred to the new cabin, Juan made coffee and poured all of them a cup. The youngsters stayed outside where Mateo showed them the new corral and the space they had outlined with small rocks for his mother's vegetable garden.

Mateo had learned some English and was able to get some information across to Taylor and Lorne, who had decided they needed to learn to speak Spanish. Next year they could take classes on it at school. They thought that would be neat so they could teach their parents to speak it too.

At length, Curtis told Juan and Lucila, "I won't be able to come back until Thursday, but I have an idea Chance will come out after he gets off work. I don't know if he will come out every day or not, and I don't know what day Woody has off this week. Whatever day it is, I'm fairly sure he will come with Chance. Maybe they can help build the other corral and a round pen. Or at least get the wood cut and brought in. I'm going to check with Marvin Hodges again and see when he can drill a well at this corral. It will be on the outside of the corral with a spout attached to it to run water into the tank I'll pick up to set in the corral."

Juan turned his head and looked toward the corral and nodded in understanding.

* * * * *

On the way home, Megan commented, "That sure is a pretty cabin. You menfolk did a really good job with it."

Curtis glanced at his wife and smiled. He was glad she approved of it.

"Dad, can we take Spanish classes next year in school?" Taylor asked.

"I think that's a good idea, Taylor. Maybe we can make it a family affair. Your mom and I need to learn it too," he answered.

"Boy, that sounds like fun!" Lorne popped off. "Just think, all of us learning Spanish at the same time!"

His young voice was filled with excitement, and his eyes sparkled.

"Maybe we could hire a tutor this summer," Megan suggested. "It would be great to be able to visit with Lucila in a language we both know."

* * * * *

Chance went to the cabins all three weekday afternoons. He and Juan cleared the trail they used to reach the grave sites on Trail Number Four. Mateo used a hand rake to rake the limbs and trash from their road as Chance and Juan cleared away stones to make the trail wider and easier to drive on. Once they were satisfied with it, they went on west to cut more trees for corrals and sheds. Chance cut them to the size they needed and hauled the cut logs in the back of his truck to the cabin area. Then they started clearing a space for the first shed. Chance liked Mateo and his siblings and began calling them as his nephews and niece, and they in turn called him Uncle Chance. Chance loved kids, so Mateo calling him Uncle Chance did not bother him. In fact—he admitted to himself—he rather enjoyed it.

That Wednesday he bought new cots and put them in the old cabin to replace those they had given Juan for the bedrooms where their kids slept. Most of what had been bought for their first cabin, Curtis had bought, and Chance felt like it was time for him and his brother Woody to chip in and help out. Curtis also paid Mr. Hodges for the water well for Juan's cabin, so he figured he and Woody would pay for the one for the corral. He would mention that to Woody next time he saw him.

That night, he called Curtis and told him what he and Juan had done. He asked Curtis if he was going to Pueblo the next morning to pick up some more meat to bring home and take some to Juan and Lucila.

"I can do that," Curtis told him. "I can go on out to Juan's and take his to him."

"Have you called Mr. Hodges yet about the well for the corral?" Chance asked.

"No. Why?"

"Woody and I are going to pay him for the next one. Woody doesn't know that yet, but he will," Chance told him.

"Well, you'll get no argument from me on that one," Curtis replied.

"It wouldn't do you any good if I did. You've paid out more than your fair share already in helping Juan and his family," Chance told his brother.

* * * * *

Curtis welcomed the trip to Pueblo the next morning. Ron Belcher gave him a warm welcome when he entered the Meat Processing Plant.

"Hey, man! Long time no see. How's everything going out your way?" he asked.

Curtis filled Belcher in on what had been going on since he and his brothers had moved the Diego's out to their cabin, concluding, "You'll have to get yourself out there one of these days."

"Why don't I just follow you out there now?" Belcher asked as he helped Curtis fill a large box with meat from the locker.

"That's fine with me. I'm going to stop by my place first and let my wife fill her freezer. Then if you want to, you can leave your vehicle at my place and ride out to the cabins with me," Curtis told him.

"Sounds good to me," Ron Belcher agreed.

He closed his shop and followed Curtis Demming back to Walsenburg.

When he unloaded the meat so Megan could take what she wanted of it, she greeted Ron Belcher also.

Noting that Belcher had parked his truck out of the way on the driveway, Curtis told Megan, "Ron may be spending the night with us. We're going to take the rest of this meat out to Lucila and stay and help Chance for a while."

"Wonderful. I'll have supper ready when you get in. Bring Chance here for supper too," she answered.

"I'll tell him you said so," he teased with a grin.

Ron Belcher looked in awe at the cabins and corrals that had been built on the Demming place. He was as glad to see the Diego family as they were to see him. Curtis carried the meat inside for Lucila and showed Belcher the inside of their house.

"Juan and Mateo helped build this one."

"It's beautiful," Belcher commented.

He followed Curtis outside as he went to look for Chance, who had been busy laying a frame for a shed. Chance came forward and shook hands with Belcher as he welcomed him.

"What you and Juan have done the past few days looks good, Chance," Curtis complimented his brother, telling Chance that Megan was expecting him for supper.

"How much more do you plan to build out here?" Ron Belcher asked.

Chance told him they had two sheds they were going to build and at least one more corral, and added that after that, they would probably build a fence around Lucila's garden area to keep the wildlife out of it.

32

That evening at supper, Ron Belcher brought up the subject of coal and asked them if they checked to see if any of the old coal mines might be somewhere on their property.

"We hadn't considered that. And the only coal the boys found while collecting rocks were small pieces along the edge of the little creek that runs through the area we call Trail Number Four," Curtis told him.

"You know Walsenburg is said to have been built by coal. And for many years, it was the main production center west of the Mississippi River. As far as I know, there are still some active coal mines here," Belcher informed them.

"Is that right?" Chance asked in surprise. He had not heard rumors of coal mining in this area, except for what their brother Woody had told them a few months back, and he wasn't aware there were still active coal mines nearby or that Walsenburg had its beginning as a coal mining town.

"That's interesting," Curtis said.

He had not known that about Walsenburg either.

He and his brothers had bought their land because of the beauty of the area and because it reminded them a lot of the area they had grown up in. Most people no longer used coal for their fireplaces or for the cookstoves, so he doubted there were many active coal mines around now. And like his brother Chance, he knew only what Woody had told them earlier. Curtis thought it might be a good idea to check it out on their property and see if there happened by chance to be any old coal mines that they needed to be fenced off to keep his sons from getting hurt in them. They were still young enough to know no fear of things.

"I thought Woody told us Walsenburg was started and named for a man called Fred Walsen," Curtis stated.

Ron Belcher smiled and told him, "Originally it was. It was later changed to its present name of Walsenburg."

"So how many mines do you think are still operating?" Chance asked.

"I don't know exactly," Belcher confessed. "But offhand, I would guess there are probably a half a dozen and maybe not that many. But it still might be a good idea when you have time to check the rest of your property. You just never know what you may find."

"That will have to wait until we get through with the cabin area and find some livestock to take out there. Once we get situated, then we will most assuredly want to inspect the rest of the place," Curtis replied.

Chance agreed.

Ron Belcher spent the weekend with Megan and Curtis and seemed to enjoy the chatter the boys made and what the Diego children made also. At their cabin homesite, he helped where he could to get the first shed built. Mateo, Taylor, and Lorne helped where they could also. That was mostly carrying logs to the shed for the men or helping hold one in place while one of the men notched it and nailed it in place. But it gave the boys a sense of pride to know they had helped build the shed.

"Chance, keep an eye out for a good used pickup for Juan," Curtis told his brother. "He needs a way to haul wood for his fireplace and whatever other things he needs to do. And since you're handy with a rifle, you might look for one for Juan. That will let him kill what meat he needs and also he'll have something to kill snakes and bobcats with."

Chance's response was a quiet 'okay'.

* * * * *

Two weeks later, with the Demming brothers helping out around their regular jobs, the second shed stood proudly several yards to the east of the original cabin facing south. This one was longer than the first and would be used as a garage to house their vehicles whenever they came to work or to hunt and would give Juan a place to store the vehicle Chance would eventually find for him.

They were teaching him to drive little by little by letting him drive their own vehicles while they were there to supervise. He learned fast, and soon they were able to get a driving manual for him to study for his license.

The following week, Chance drove out to the cabin site in a black pickup.

"Juan, if you like this pickup, I'll get it for you," he told the Mexican.

Juan Diego couldn't hold back the tears that filled his eyes, and he stated, "Senor, you and your brothers have done far too much for me and my family already."

Chance gave Juan a somber look and told him, "We were glad to do it, Juan. And remember, we told you we needed your help out here. We still do. But having your own vehicle will allow you to be able to go to town for groceries and whatever else you and your family might need. Plus, you will be able to gather and bring home firewood as you need it. We will still be around now and then because Woody and Curtis are looking for horses and mules to buy. And they might stumble on to a milk cow for you too. So if you'll drive me back to town, we can get this signed over to you and you can drive yourself back home."

"Thank you, Senor," Juan said before he went around to get into the vehicle.

On the way to town, Chance asked Juan if he knew how to shoot a gun. Juan told him he had shot a rifle years ago when he was younger, but he hadn't shot one since.

"Okay. You're going to need one, not only for predators but for snakes too. So I will get you one, and we'll practice with it until you feel comfortable using it," Chance told him.

Chance stopped at the Sheriff's Office to see about Juan taking the driving test. He was able to get an officer who took Juan out to the black pickup and rode with him during the driving test, which Juan passed. The officer then took Juan inside and filled out his license for him and printed a copy for Juan to keep on his person until his license was mailed to him. Chance told the officer to call him at the Auto Dealership when Juan's license was ready and he would take it out to him, explaining to the officer that Juan worked for him and his brothers and that there was no mailing address at the cabin site where Juan lived. The officer agreed.

At the dealership, Chance signed the paperwork, signing the black pickup over to Juan, telling him, "Now you can drive yourself back home, Juan."

After Juan left, Chance made his way to the Mercantile and asked the clerk, "What do you have in way of Browning .30-06 rifles?"

"I don't have any Browning rifles in stock, Mr. Demming, but I can order you one," the clerk told him.

"If you wouldn't mind," Chance replied. "Order me one of those new Browning BXR .30-06 rifles I've been hearing about and also order some shells for it. Call me when they get here."

"Consider it done," the clerk said.

That Browning rifle should do anything Juan needed it to do, Chance told himself.

He called Curtis and asked if he and Woody could come for supper. Then he called Woody to come to Curtis's place for supper.

The nephews were excited about having their uncles for supper and greeted them with an excited "Hi, Uncle Woody!" and "Hi, Uncle Chance!"

"What have you two onery boys been up to?" Woody asked them.

"We learned how to ride our bikes!" Lorne told him.

The importance of that was not lost on Uncle Woody who responded, "Good deal!"

Not to be left out, Taylor told his uncles that they were going to get to learn Spanish that summer.

"Hey, that's good. That may be something all of us need to do," Woody told him.

Curtis helped his wife set the table. Now Chance told them about getting a pickup for Juan, getting him his driving license, and ordering him a rifle.

"Sounds like you have had a busy afternoon," Curtis commented.

"I didn't want to bring this up in front of Belcher, but him talking about the coal mines got me to wondering if those graves might be graves of miners instead of Indians."

"I hadn't thought of that," Curtis said.

"Nor I," Woody confessed. "And you could quite possibly be right."

"I think this weekend, we need to go ahead and fence that area," Chance told them.

His brothers agreed with him.

"Another thing, we need to start paying Juan a little every month now so he and Lucila can buy their own groceries and the things they think they need," Woody said.

"How would three hundred a month be? We can help him set up a bank account so that people won't be wondering where he gets his money from."

"How about six hundred, two hundred apiece from each of us for now. We can raise it later on. We could set up his bank account the first week of May. That's coming up in a few days," Curtis replied.

Chance agreed with him, and after giving it a few minutes of thought, Woody finally agreed too.

33

The month of May was spent in building the other two corrals and clearing the area around them and the cabin site of tree stubs and other types of debris and making the road to the pasture more accessible for their vehicles.

Once that was done, with the help of the growing boys, they sent for Marvin Hodges to get the well drilled near the first corral. Woody brought out a water tank for them to use in that corral, along with two ninety-four-gallon tanks for the other two corrals. He also bought and brought along some heavy-duty water hoses by which to fill the smaller tanks by way of attaching them to the spout at the first tank.

Marvin Hodges was amazed at the improvements at the cabin site.

"You folks have turned this into a beautiful home site," the elder Hodges said with admiration.

They showed him where they wanted the second well drilled. He marked it and began to set up for drilling it. Hodges then asked them if they could help with it because his son had to work. They did, and a few hours later, water poured into the waiting tank.

"You wouldn't happen to know where we could get a milk cow and maybe a couple of gentle horses, would you?" Curtis asked him.

"Not right off hand," Hodges told him. "But I'll keep an ear out, and if I come up with something, I'll let you know."

"Thanks," Curtis replied.

"Have you checked the newspaper ads lately? There might be something in there," Hodges suggested.

"I haven't, but I'll pick up a paper when I go home this evening," Curtis assured him.

Between work and helping his brothers and Juan Diego build up the cabin site, he hadn't thought about looking at the newspaper ads. He had an idea his brothers hadn't either. Now that they had some place to keep animals, the Diego's definitely needed a milk cow. Two reasons he could think of quickly were milk for the kids to drink and milk for Lucila to use in her cooking. Plus, if they could get a Guernsey or a Jersey, Lucila would have cream to make butter with and buttermilk for cakes and pancakes.

He was glad Lucila hadn't asked if she could have chickens for eggs. Chickens would draw predators—coyotes, wolves, racoons, and the like. Snakes were also known to invade chicken coops. They didn't need any of that type of company at the cabins, theirs or Juan's. Besides, it was less expensive to buy eggs in town than to have to buy grain for the chickens.

* * * * *

That evening on his way home, Curtis Demming stopped and bought a newspaper. Later, when he scanned through the ads on the newspaper pages, he did not see any ads for milk cows for sale, but he did see an ad for an upcoming livestock sale the first Saturday of every month. He would keep that in mind and maybe he could take a Saturday off to see what came through the sale ring. It would give him a chance to talk to other farmers and ranchers about what were the best horses and mules to buy, and if there were actually a demand for mules in their area. He fathomed maybe he could find out where he might get a milk cow. It was something to think about to him.

Taylor interrupted his thinking by telling him that he and Lorne were off that Friday from school because of a teachers' meeting.

"Would it be all right if we go with you out to the cabins?" he asked.

Curtis looked at his eldest son. Taylor was growing in leaps and bounds now and was several inches taller than he had been when the building had begun at the cabin site.

Now he was a gangly teenager that would fill out more rapidly as the months went by.

"Taylor, how would you boys like to go to the Lathrop State Park this weekend?" he asked his son.

"Hey! That would be great, Dad," Taylor replied with enthusiasm.

"Well then, you and Lorne pack a backpack and be ready to leave Friday morning. I'll go tell your mom," his dad told him.

Megan was fixing a casserole for their supper. She looked up as her husband entered the kitchen. He was all smiles, and she was anxious to know what he was thinking.

"Megan, the boys have a three-day weekend because of a teachers' meeting, so I thought we'd take them out to the Lathrop State Park. We all need a break and that would give us a chance to relax for a few hours," he told her.

"That sounds like a wonderful idea, Curtis," she replied. "Maybe later on this summer, we can take in the Spanish Peaks Park too."

"It's an idea," he agreed. "They're both old enough to have great memories of the places they get to go. I'm not so sure you haven't slipped a little bit of Miracle-Gro in their meals. They're growing like little weeds!"

Megan Demming laughed at her husband.

"No Miracle-Gro," she assured him.

"They're both at that age where they grow in spurts every few days. And it won't be long before we'll have to buy them new clothes."

"I figured we'd leave Friday morning and come back Sunday afternoon," he told her.

* * * * *

Lathrop State Park, only five miles west of Walsenburg, was every bit as beautiful as some of the local people had told them it was. They walked through much of it, marveling at the awesome scenery, some of which they took pictures of. They walked along the Hogback Trail, a loop claiming 1.3 miles of beauty and housing One-seed Juniper, Gamble Oak, and Pinyon Pine trees, and runs along the top of a hogback ridge, providing views to the north, west, and south offering the beauty of the Spanish Peaks to the west of it, and also the Greenhorn Mountains—sometimes called the "Wet Mountain"—views to the northwest of it. The Sangre de Cristo Mountains were not to be left out in its beauty.

There were a host of different plants, including Prickly Pear Cactus growing with awesome areas that also sponsored Pinon and Juniper trees. Later, Taylor and Lorne enjoyed the water slide at the playground area.

There were signs along for the Boating area that also featured fishing and water skiing on the two lakes that helped enhance the beauty of Lathrop State Park—the Martin Lake and the Horseshoe Lake.

As the day drew to a close, Curtis told the boys they needed to get home for now and make another day of it tomorrow. He had not realized this beautiful park was so close to Walsenburg, but since it was, there was no sense in him booking a motel when they could sleep in their own beds and return to the park tomorrow. The boys enjoyed their outing and chattered excitedly about it all the way home.

34

It was Monday all over again. Curtis Demming was considering going to the upcoming livestock sale that Saturday. His thoughts were interrupted by Woody. He hadn't heard Woody come into the house.

"What's up?" he asked his brother.

"Got a call from Paul Dunhurst today," Woody told him as he seated himself into the stuffed chair across Curtis. "He and Krigler want to come out this Saturday to look over the burial site one more time. Krigler thinks they may have been from an old culture that roamed near central Texas and on up through the panhandle and possibly also into regions of Colorado. So he wants to look at them again."

"He took a ton of photos last time he and Dunhurst were here. Why does he need more?" Curtis asked.

"I don't have any idea," Woody told him.

"Have you talked to Chance?" Curtis asked.

"I called him. But you know how he is. He had something going on, and all he told me was 'okay.' We'll meet them at the gas station Saturday morning," Woody replied.

* * * * *

They met the Archaeologists at the gas station that Saturday and had them follow them out to the burial ground. There Charles Krigler took out the photos he had taken the last time he and Paul Dunhurst had been here. He laid out a white cloth and spread the photos across it and studied them for several minutes.

"I went down to central and northwestern Texas after finding out that was at one time an area occupied by a cultural people that are thought to have lived there between the BC 800 and 900 on up until 1300's," Charles Krigler told the men. "That categorizes them as prehistoric. And that's what I believe these are. They are known as cairns and not graves or burial grounds, even though that's what we commonly and mistakenly call them today."

"Really?" Curtis asked in astonishment. "Prehistoric, huh? No wonder there were never any records of them!"

"Then the Sheriff was right when he said they might be prehistoric," Woody said.

He and Chance were as surprised at that as Curtis was. It showed in their faces.

"Here, I have some photos of the ones I took pictures of in Texas. Let me show them to you."

With that, he moved to the vehicle he and Dunhurst had driven, took out a briefcase that he deposited on the back of the vehicle next to the pictures of these graves, opened it, and drew out a stack of other photos that he spread out beside the rest. It was uncanny how much the ones from Texas looked like the ones on the Demming property in Colorado. Had they not been dated, Krigler's photos might have been thought to have come from the same burial sites.

"That's unreal! They could be the same graves, except they are in different places," Chance stated.

"That's a fact!" Woody agreed.

"So will you be able to record them?" Curtis asked.

He found it awesome that if they hadn't known better, all the photos Charles Krigler had brought with him and shown them could have been of the same graves and from the same area.

Charles Krigler allowed himself a slight smile. "They will be in my files as having been recorded from my own research, but that's all I can do with them because of them turning up as prehistoric cairns. I'm sorry, gentlemen."

"I'm sorry, too," Paul Dunhurst told them. "But this has given me something I can incorporate into my classroom lectures and assignments at the college, and for that, I want to thank you."

Woody spoke up then, saying, "And we want to thank you guys for checking into it for us. We will go ahead and fence it now if for no other reason than to keep my nephews and the hired hand's kids out of it. Meanwhile, you gentlemen are welcome any time you care to come out."

The eagle had watched them from his perch in a nearby tree. Today, however, he allowed their presence in his domain without scolding them.

"We might just do that. You folks have built up quite a nice place there where the cabins are," Krigler commented.

"Your hired hand is a Mexican, isn't he?" Dunhurst asked.

"Yes he is. We were told about him last fall and told he is honest, which he has proven to be. We found him and his family living in a rundown little shanty outside of Pueblo, cold and starving. We reinforced the shanty for him, but when winter hit in earnest, we moved them into our cabin, and he later helped us build his cabin. Plus, he helped build the sheds and the corrals," Curtis replied.

"I see. Well, good luck, and I hope everything works out for you," Dunhurst told him.

Both he and Krigler shook hands with the Demming brothers before getting into their vehicle.

Watching them leave, Curtis said aloud, "Prehistoric! If that don't beat all!"

"Yeah," Chance said. "I would have never guessed it."

"Me neither. That's almost unreal," Woody commented. "You could have bowled me over with a feather."

They stood for several minutes digesting what the State Archaeologist had told them and shown them with his photographs of the different grave areas in Texas and the one here.

"One thing about it, Krigler went all out to find out about these graves for us. And as he said he's done all he can do," Woody told his brothers. "They told me in Denver that grave sites that were considered prehistoric were not able to be put on record. And Krigler said these are prehistoric. I still think it would be a good idea to fence this site and mark it just so we will know it's a prehistoric site."

Both of his brothers agreed with him.

"Woody, why don't you make a sign for it as prehistoric burial cairns? You're good at designing things," Curtis responded. "In a couple of weeks, we can come out and fence it and attach the sign to the fence."

Woody agreed, and they walked to their vehicles and left the area.

35

Woody sought out a large, fairly flat stone on which to make the sign they would exhibit at the burial ground on their property. He cleaned it and sanded it smooth on one side. Using a piece of chalk, he carefully printed the words "Prehistoric Burial Cairns."

Using his Dremel tools, he took extreme care in etching out the printed words he had drawn on the face of the stone. He ground them half an inch deep so they could proudly announce to the world what it would so honorably guard to eternity. Then he took time to polish its face, bringing out a beautiful light brown that made the words on it stand out.

When he finished, he called his brothers to come look at it. It passed their inspection with flying colors.

"When we fence it, let's use a chain-link fence," Chance suggested. "The gate can open inward for us to go in and clean up around it when it needs it and can be secured with a lock the rest of the time. We can each have a key to the lock. And we can place that stone directly in front of the gate. I don't think anyone will bother it."

"That sounds like a good idea, Chance. I think it's highly unlikely that anyone outside our family and the Archaeology men will ever see it. But you never know. To say the least, after we have all passed away, anyone possessing the property in the future won't have to guess what they are or go through what Charles Krigler went through in finding out what they are." Curtis said.

"Why don't we fence it this weekend—say Saturday—and get that done and over with?" Woody asked.

Curtis and Chance both told him okay.

"I'll pick up the fence and accessories when I get off work Friday," Chance told them. "We can get Juan to help us. It shouldn't take more than a couple of hours to be done with it."

"I'll come by and help you load that rock, Woody. I don't think you loaded and unloaded that by yourself," Curtis told Woody.

"No I didn't," Woody admitted. "A friend of mine helped with it. But I don't want him knowing where it's going. I didn't tell him what it is for. So yeah, if you wouldn't mind, I would appreciate the help."

"You got anything cold to drink?" Chance asked.

"There's a six-pack of Budweiser in the refrigerator," Woody answered. "Help yourself."

* * * * *

That Saturday, they all drove out to the cabins where Chance had Juan ride with him out to the grave site.

They unloaded the lengths of chain-link fence and worked it out from the gate pieces on the front to the corners, then worked one side, the back, and the other side back to its corner at the front. Chance had extra keys made for the lock, and after he snapped it in place on the gate, he gave each of his brothers a key for it. Then he and Woody carefully lifted the stone marker and set it in place in front of the gate. They stepped back to where Curtis and Juan were standing and admired their handiwork for several minutes.

"Juan, we don't want your kids anywhere around this," Curtis told Juan. "My boys have already been told they are not to bother it."

"Si, Senor, I will tell them and see to it they do not bother it," Juan assured him.

Chance looked at his brothers and then at Juan. His eyes began to twinkle and he asked, "Why don't we have a barbeque down at the cabins tomorrow afternoon for all of us?"

He got no argument. Only smiles and nods of agreement from all of them. He thought his nephews would probably be delighted. He couldn't remember the last time he had fixed barbeque for any of them. He didn't know how long it had been since Juan and Lucila had eaten barbeque either, if ever. It would be a treat for all of them. He himself would fix potato salad to go with it and start the barbeque meat early. He knew his sister-in-law Megan would dream up something to make and bring, and Woody would bring something, maybe some beer and some kind of drinks for the kids.

When Curtis Demming got home, he told his wife about the barbeque he and his brothers had planned for the following day.

"Oh, that's wonderful Curtis!" she replied. "I'll make some cookies to take along and then see about making a green bean casserole put together."

"Where are the boys?" he asked

"They're both down at the baseball practice field with their friends," she told him.

"Good. I'm going to take a shower, and then we may go down to the Busy Bee for supper," he replied.

While he showered, Megan mixed up a double batch of chocolate chip cookies. She sat them in the refrigerator while she mixed the green bean casserole for tomorrow's barbeque. That too she put in the refrigerator to cook after they got home from the café.

She was delighted her husband was taking her out to eat. It had been a long time since the two of them had been out together alone. They would be home before Taylor and Lorne came home from the baseball field, and they could eat sandwiches and chips later.

The Busy Bee wasn't too crowded. They sat at a table about midway down the café. They ordered the day's special, along with a glass of sherry, and enjoyed every bite.

They were home a good twenty minutes before Taylor and Lorne came through the door. Megan put the green bean casserole in the oven and took out the cookie sheets to use after the casserole was done.

"Something smells good, Mom!" Taylor said.

She smiled and told her sons of the barbeque out at the cabins the next day. "So you boys wash up and fix yourselves some sandwiches to eat. Daddy and I went out to eat earlier. I've still got a double batch of cookies to bake this evening."

"That sounds like fun," Lorne told her. "Anything I can do to help, Mom?"

"No, honey, but you boys need to go ahead and get your showers as soon as your Dad gets through with his," she told them.

"Will Uncle Woody and Uncle Chance be there too?" Taylor asked her.

She smiled at him and asked him when he had ever known his uncles to miss out on a barbeque. They laughed with her. The boys then went to their rooms to put up their baseball gloves and pick out the clothes they would wear tomorrow. They both looked forward to getting to be with Juan's family again. Mateo, Manuela, and Luis had become their friends.

＊ ＊ ＊ ＊ ＊

The next morning found all of them in a mood of merriment. As soon as Megan put her casserole and cookies in a box and set them inside the truck, they were ready to go. Curtis stopped by the gas station and bought a bag of ice to take with them for the drinks he knew Woody was bringing.

Chance was already there when Curtis got there, and Juan was helping set up the grill.

"The one thing I forgot was a folding table to set the food on," Chance told his brother.

"I can go get one, Chance. I'll have it back here by the time you get the ribs done," Curtis volunteered. "Woody should be here before I get back."

He met Woody on his way into town, stopped long enough to tell his brother where he was going, and went on to Walsenburg. At the Mercantile, he found tables but not one the length he was hoping to find, so he bought two shorter ones that, when set end to end, would suffice. He also found a small wash tub that would do to put the ice he had bought earlier in, providing it hadn't melted by the time he got back. That thought prompted him to stop and buy another bag of ice one his way back to the cabins.

Chance had already put the ribs on the grill. He and Woody off loaded the tables and set them up while he and Juan set about putting the drinks into the tub and filling it with ice.

Lucila made homemade tortillas to go with the rest of their meal. Chance opened the grill and turned the ribs over and spread more barbeque sauce on them with his brush. They would need to cook a while longer, but that gave the youngsters more time to play the game they were engaged in at present. It looked Greek to him, but they were whooping and playing and laughing and having fun.

Chance loved kids, and once in a while it pained him that he didn't have any of his own. But by the same token, he had yet to find a woman he wanted to settle down with. Until that time, he would just have to settle for enjoying someone else's kids.

Birds were chirping merrily, and Chance saw the shadow of the eagle as it flew overhead checking out the human creatures. He looked up to see where it was going. It flew further west and out of sight. He assumed it was hunting its own lunch.

Curtis spread a sheet across the tables to set the food on, and the women began bringing the food and setting it on the tables. When they were done, he had Woody help him lift the tub of ice and sodas and set it at one end of the tables.

"I guess the women can have the chairs, and the rest of us can fill our plates and set on the ground," Curtis commented.

Chance began taking the ribs off the grill and setting the foil roaster pans on the table. Curtis thought to himself that it looked like they could feed half the county. But he kept his thoughts to himself.

Megan and Lucila called the children and let them begin filling their plates and getting the sodas they wanted from the tub. They told them to find a place and sit down and eat. Taylor led them to the rock fence they started at the garden spot. It was high enough to sit on and level enough to sit their drinks on.

Megan and Lucila filled plates and selected drinks and sat in the two chairs at one end of the table across each other. The men filled plates and picked out drinks and found places to sit on the ground a little ways away from the grill. It was a good day for the cookout because the day was clear with only a slight breeze blowing and the temperature had warmed up too, making it to where they only needed to wear long-sleeved shirts and blouses outside.

Woody told the men as they began eating that he believed he knew where they could buy a milk cow.

"Where?" Curtis asked.

"There's an old man who lives a few miles south of Walsenburg who is planning to sell his cows," Woody told them. "If you guys want to go with me, we can go look at them tomorrow."

"I have to work tomorrow. But Juan and Chance can go with you," Curtis told him.

"I get off work at eleven tomorrow," Chance said.

"Well then, Juan, if you want to go, I'll come get you in the morning and then swing by and pick up Chance and we'll go see if we can buy some cows," Woody offered.

"Si, Senor Woody. I would love to go," Juan replied.

"Check them out good, Woody. We need good cows, not rejects. And we don't want old cows either. Juan needs one to milk and maybe one or two that will calve later on. So don't buy just anything," Curtis cautioned his brother.

"We will," Chance answered. "I wouldn't want our dad to come up out of his grave and whip all of us. And you know he would if we were to buy sorry cows."

When they were through eating, the men helped take the leftover food to Lucila's kitchen where she and Megan found smaller dishes to put the food in. Then Megan helped Lucila clean and put up the dishes they had eaten from and the ones they had removed the leftover food from.

It had been a good afternoon for all of them. Taylor and Lorne weren't ready to leave. They would have both liked to have been able to stay longer, but they knew they had better get in the pickup when their dad told them it was time to be getting home.

36

The place Woody had been told about where the cows were for sale was near Cuchara, some miles south of Walsenburg. They drove through awesome beauty as they ventured toward Cuchara and the Cucharas River Valley which lay at the base of the eastern side of the Sangre de Cristo Mountains on their left. They marveled at the Cucharas River that ran along the edge of the town itself.

Woody stopped at the bar to ask directions to the place that had advertised the cows for sale.

"You must mean old man Gibbins," the barkeep said.

"I don't know his name," Woody admitted. "I was told a man down in this area had some cows for sale, and we are looking for some milk cows, which I was told he has."

"He's a trader. So do be careful what you buy from him, Mister," the barkeep advised.

"Thanks. Can you tell us how to get to his place?" Woody asked.

"When you get to the south end of town, turn right and drive about four miles, and then turn left onto a dirt road. From there, it's about three-quarters of a mile to his place. But you may have to pay close attention because that area is forested with Ponderosa pine trees, and they tend to hide his place from view," the bar keep told hm.

"Thanks," Woody replied.

As they got into the vehicle again, Chance commented, "Cuchara, population 140, according to the sign back there."

Woody and Juan both smiled at him.

"Chance, you might get lost in a city that big!" Woody teased him.

Following the directions the barkeep had given them, they also found a sign that said "San Isabel National Forrest" on it. Ponderosa pine became more numerous as they neared the turnoff to old man Gibbins's place. The driveway was dirt but fairly wide and formed a semicircle to the house. It looked to be built mostly of wooden logs, with other accents built on.

The old man heard them drive up and now came out of the house to greet them. He looked to be in his seventies. Dressed in Western garb, he gave the impression of having once been a cowboy.

Woody, Chance, and Juan got out of the pickup to greet him. Woody introduced himself, his brother, and Juan to him and related to him they had heard he had some cows to sell. The old man introduced himself as Hiram Gibbins and told them to follow him.

He took them around the side of the house, past an old wire chicken coop, and on around to the corrals several feet further behind his house. He pointed to half a dozen cows in one corral who were lazily chomping on a bale of hay.

"These are what I'm aimin' to sell," he told them, as the three men looked at them.

"Mind if I go in the corral with them?" Chance asked.

"Go ahead, young feller. I always wanted to look over what I was intendin' to buy. I've found that if you look 'em over good before you buy, you don't come home with somethin' you didn't want," Mr. Gibbins told him.

"Any of them giving milk?" Woody asked him.

"That brindle-color cow and the red cow are the two you want if you want milk," Gibbins answered.

Juan climbed into the corral with Chance to look at the two cows the old man had said were giving milk. He and Chance looked them over good. Both seemed to be healthy and both younger than the other four. He bent his knees and looked at the udders on both cows. The red cow seemed to have been milked recently. He mentioned that to Chance.

"How much do you want for the red cow?" Chance asked, turning to look at Gibbins.

Hiram Gibbins took his hat off and smoothed back his hair and replaced the hat.

"Could you come up with sixty dollars for her?"

"She seems all right. She's gentle. She looks to have been milked recently. Does she give much milk?" Chance asked.

"I milked her this morning, and she gives about two quarts of milk per milking. And I must say, you gentlemen picked the best of the bunch," Gibbins returned with a gentle laugh.

"In that case, we'll take her. You want to help us get her into the back of the pickup?" Chance answered.

They loaded the cow, and for lack of stock rails, they tied together some poles and made a temporary stock rack in the back of Woody's pickup. Gibbins put an armload of hay in the front of the bed of the pickup for the cow. Satisfied then that she would ride, Woody paid Hiram Gibbins for her.

They all shook hands with the old man and thanked him.

"You gentlemen come back when you can," Gibbins told them.

Woody rolled down the window on his side of the pickup and asked Gibbins if he would keep an eye out for some mules and horses for them.

"I'll do 'er. I need your phone number so's I can call you," he answered.

Woody gave him the information and thanked him again.

"Can I get a receipt for this cow?" Woody asked.

As honest as the old man seemed to be, Woody knew there were people who would have let him drive off and then phoned the local authorities and reported the cow stolen.

The old man grinned at him and told him, "Sure . . . if you have something to make one out on."

Chance produced a small tablet and an ink pen from the glove department of the pickup and handed it to his brother, who in turned handed it to Hiram Gibbins. Gibbins made out a handwritten bill of sale, dated it, signed his name to it, and handed it back to Woody.

Again, Woody thanked him and backed his pickup carefully out of the driveway and on to the road. He could have driven forward since this was a semicircle drive. But for some unknown reason, he wanted to be where they could keep an eye on Gibbins as they left his place. Once away from the place, he asked Chance if he had experienced a similar feeling. He had, and so had Juan.

"He seems friendly enough and honest enough, but I wouldn't trust him as far as I could throw him," Chance commented.

They stopped back by the local bar, ordered a beer, and had the barkeep come outside and look at the cow they had purchased.

He studied the cow for a few minutes then stated, "I hope you got a receipt for her."

"We did. And I guess we better get her home," Woody said.

The barkeep bade them goodbye with an invitation to come again sometime.

Chance stopped and turned and asked the barkeep, "Say, do you know where we could get one of the old icebox refrigerators?"

"People haven't used those forever," the barkeep told him. "Let me look in the back. The owner never throws away anything. So there may still be a couple of them out there."

Chance followed the man to the back storage room. Way in the back in a corner was one of the old iceboxes. The barkeep showed it to Chance. It looked to be in pretty good shape and still had shelves inside. It wouldn't take much to clean it up so Lucila could store food that needed refrigerated inside it.

"How much would you want for that?" Chance asked him.

"Let me call my boss right quick," the barkeep said and went to the front of the bar to make his call.

In a few minutes, he came back, telling Chance that his boss said they could have it, and offered to help get it to the truck.

Woody nudged the cow over and slid the icebox into a corner at the back of his truck.

"Have you got something we can put around this to keep it steady?" he asked.

"Let me look. There may be some twine or wire or something in the back of the bar," the bar keep said.

He returned shortly with some short pieces of cotton rope.

"Maybe if you tie these together, there will be enough to go around it," he said.

On the way back to the cabins, they stopped by Curtis's house to show him and Megan the cow before taking it on to the country.

Both Curtis and Megan thought Woody had done okay buying this cow for Juan and Lucila.

Megan walked to the ice box and asked, "What's that?"

Curtis put an arm around her and answered, "That's an icebox, Megan. In the old days, people had to buy blocks of ice and set them to one side in it, and they used the other side to put refrigerated foods in. The ice kept the food cool, at least until it melted, and that takes a while because it is cool inside the box."

"Oh, maybe we can find one for our cabin," she replied.

The nephews were not to be left out. They looked on the cow with excitement on their young faces.

"Can we ride out to the cabins with you, Uncle Woody?" Taylor asked.

His Uncle Woody smiled and told him to ask his dad.

Lorne spoke up with, "Can we, Dad? Please! We won't get in the way—I promise!"

Curtis agreed the boys could go. He and his wife both smiled at their eagerness. It was not only a ride to the cabins; it was more wanting to be with their uncles and to see Juan's kids and play with them for a few minutes. He knew his brothers would take care of them, and if need be, their uncles would make them mind too.

37

Megan reminded Curtis that they needed to go to Pueblo and get some meat that weekend. She was down to the last few packages in their home freezer. He nodded and told her okay.

"I might ought to see if I can find a few bales of hay for that cow while we're out and about," he mentioned. "There's grass out in the country but not much up close. Juan may have to fashion a halter for her and take her out where he can stay with her for a few hours a day while she grazes. That is if he plans to have milk for the kids."

"Maybe you could find him something to cut some of that tall grass on that meadow on the north side or maybe the one out on the west side near that old road. He could cut it and use a hand rake to pile it up, then load it in the back of his pickup and bring it to the corral for the cow."

"Well, now, aren't you a smart one? I hadn't thought of that," Curtis admitted.

"We can take our time and look for what you want before we pick up the meat," she suggested.

Curtis stopped at the Walsenburg Mercantile and asked the clerk if he carried weed whips and pitch forks and rakes or sickles.

The clerk could only provide him with a rake and a pitchfork. Curtis paid him and thanked him. He carried the tools out to his pickup and laid them in the back. He asked Megan if she needed anything before they went on to Pueblo.

"Not that I can think of," she told him.

In Pueblo, they found a farm store where Curtis was able to find the sickle and weed whip he was looking for, along with some other tools such as crowbars and some crescent wrenches he didn't have. The store was old and fairly rundown and looked as if at one time it may have been a warehouse for the CF&I Steel Mill. Steel was the prime marketing product in Pueblo for a number of years. Curtis was glad to find the tools he needed, but he was just as glad to leave the place.

He drove across town to the Meat Processing Plant to get boxes of meat for both them and Diego's. When he and Megan first entered the shop, they didn't see Ron Belcher. So Curtis raised his voice and called the man's name. He waited a few minutes and called again.

Ron Belcher came to the front, pleased to see Curtis Demming and his wife.

"How is everything out at your place?" he asked.

"Good, I think. We have Juan and his family completely moved into their own cabin now. My brothers bought a milk cow for them yesterday," Curtis told him. "My brother Curtis taught him how to drive and took him to get his driver's license and found him a used pickup in good condition. He also ordered Juan a rifle to use for snakes and to keep his family in meat out there."

"Sounds like you people have truly been a blessing to him," Belcher responded.

"We kept them from freezing to death out north of town and probably from starving to death too," Curtis commented. "You'll have to come out and visit with them when you get time."

"Thanks. I will. When would be a good time?" Belcher asked.

"Anytime you want to. Someone will be there. I won't be there the first Saturday of next month because the sale barns are opening up then, and I want to see about getting a couple of mules or horses to train out at the cabins," Curtis answered. "Meantime, I need to latch on to a couple of mixed boxes of meat from the locker."

"Sure thing. I've got some boxes in the back, so come on back and get what you want out of your locker," Belcher said, heading toward the back of the shop.

They put a sizeable dent in the meat locker over the winter feeding both their own family and Juan Diego's. After filling two large boxes with frozen packages, the locker was two-thirds empty. But with Juan having a rifle now that Chance had ordered him, he would be able to kill some of his own meat now, so the meat in the locker should last until fall when Chance would once again fill it with wildlife.

When they got home, Curtis helped Megan put the meat in their freezer, leaving out a roast to thaw out for tomorrow. Afterward, they drove on out to the cabins and gave Juan the box of meat they had brought for him and Lucilla.

Curtis had Juan come with him to the west pasture, then told him he could cut grass from this meadow for the cow. Taking the sickle from the back of his truck, he began cutting grass. Juan took the weed whip and moved over to another area and began cutting with it. Curtis had only brought one pitchfork, so he moved the wrenches to the back floorboard of his truck and taking the rake began raking up the grass he'd cut into a pile, which he then lifted and loaded into the bed. When his area was done, he went to where Juan was working and raked that cut grass and loaded it into the truck.

"Juan, I'm going to leave these tools in the tool shed, and you can use them to get feed for the cow. I think we have enough for right now," he said.

"Si, Senor. That is a nice cow. I think she will like this grass," Juan smiled at Curtis.

"Well, let's get her fed," Curtis told him.

Back at the corral, the cow mooed at them and went to where they were unloading the grass for her. They stood watching her eat and soon had the rest of their families at the corral fence with them.

38

On the way home, he said to Megan, "I guess if I am going to buy horses or mules, I'd better see about getting a horse trailer."

"That would be easier than walking them home," she replied. "Where are the nearest horse sales?"

"The nearest one from here that I know of is at Monte Vista," he told her.

"How far is Monte Vista?" she asked.

"Right at a hundred miles," he answered.

Her eyes twinkled, and she smiled as she said, "Then, Curtis, I guess you'd better find a trailer to haul them home in."

He spent the next few days searching through the newspaper ads and asking his coworkers if they knew where he could find a good four-horse trailer. He checked with the trailer sales lots in Walsenburg itself. Not finding what he wanted, he finally ran an ad in the local newspaper, *The World's Journal.*

* * * * *

Sale day Saturday morning came and Chance showed up to go with Curtis to the horse sale in Monte Vista. They watched as they as they went through Fort Garland and Alamosa to see if they could spot any places that sold horse trailers. They didn't see any as they passed by, headed for Monte Vista.

The parking lot around the sale barn was nearly full. It took a few minutes for Curtis to find a place to park. They walked over to the stock pens and began walking around them to see if anything there would be suitable for their needs. As they walked by the pens, pigs oinked at them, sheep milled in their pens, and cattle bawled. Horses mostly watched them walk by, some moved to the other side of the pen away from them. Only a few of the horses were animals they might want.

As they walked back around to the office, there was a horse trailer parked near the entrance with a For Sale sign on it. Curtis and his brother looked it over. It seemed to be in good condition, even the tires. They asked some of the other men who owned it. Those men didn't seem to know, so Curtis sought out the auctioneer, who in turn came outside to look at it.

"It will have to be bought through the sale ring inside," he told them. "You gentlemen go ahead and go inside and register as buyers. By the way, what name can I put on the auction slip?"

"Demming," Curtis told him. "We live over at Walsenburg."

The auctioneer nodded and walked back to the side of the barn where Curtis had found him.

"I'll see you inside," he said as he left them.

Curtis and Chance both ordered coffee at the snack bar, then went to the office where they registered as buyers and received a numbered ticket to bid with. From there, they found seats in the bleachers inside and sat down to wait for the sale to begin.

There were vendors selling everything from ropes to ointments to gloves and saddle blankets. Between Curtis and Chance, they bought halters, brushes, gloves, and a couple of nice saddle blankets. Then they waited until the trailer came up for sale. The auctioneer asked for the owner to come to his booth. He talked to him and then told the folks they would have to go outside to bid on the trailer. Very few went outside, and it only took minutes for the Demming brothers to buy the trailer.

Later when the horses came through the sale ring, Chance was careful to pick out a nice three-year-old Appaloosa mare and later another one. After that, they went to the office to pay for their purchases. Afterward, Curtis went to get his truck so they could hook the trailer up to it. Then they had to wait awhile before they could load the mares.

"We got lucky today, Chance," Curtis commented.

"Yeah. The good Lord's been looking after us these past few days," Chance replied. "Who would have ever thought we could pick up a horse trailer right here at the sale barn? A nice one, to boot."

"Those two young mares you picked are nice too," Curtis complimented him.

It was nearing sundown by the time they were loaded and ready to head back to Walsenburg with the day's treasures.

They arrived at the cabins after dark where Juan came out to meet them.

"Look what we found today, Juan!" Curtis said.

"Si, Senor, that's a nice trailer!" Juan responded.

"Come see what we brought home in it." he said as he and Juan walked to the back of it where Chance had opened the back door to unload the mares.

He had halters and lead ropes on both, and they unloaded easily and looked about the place.

"Senors, you brought home some mighty fine horses," Juan told them.

"I don't know how well trained they are or if they have had any training. Put them in the corral, and we'll come back this weekend to look at them a little closer. Right now we need to be getting back to Walsenburg. Megan will think we deserted her," Curtis told Juan.

He backed the horse trailer to the east of where the first cabin was and stopped when Chance said "Whoa!" Chance unhooked it from the pickup and got in. Both of them waved at Juan as the pickup moved away.

Juan smiled and bid them good night.

"It's been a long day," Curtis commented. "But I think we did good."

"Among us all, we've gotten a lot done these past few days. I think, though, that will be the last business deal with that Mr. Gibbins that Woody bought the cow from," Chance told his brother. "I just don't quite trust that man. I'm glad Woody thought to get a receipt for that cow."

"Amen," Curtis agreed.

"I guess about the only thing left now is to get some feed cut for the cow and horses and get the horses worked with. Maybe we can walk Trail Number Four again and see if there's a good spot to fence off some of that grass where that stream runs through it and turn the mares in there for the next few months. That could take in that burial site since we have it fenced off. We could buy a round pen and set it up so Juan or one of us even could work with the horses there," Chance said.

"You sound more like Dad every day," Curtis told him with a smile.

He remembered their Dad thinking out loud at times while they were growing up. Always he thought ahead of things that could be done to improve their situation back then.

"Well, Curtis, right now, I think our Dad would be proud of all of us," Chance told him.

"I think he would too," Curtis Demming agreed with his brother.